THE
E~~N~~
WITCH

Daphne Paige ♡
I hope you enjoy book 2!

BOOK TWO

Daphne Paige

Copyright © 2022 by Daphne Paige

Find the author on Instagram @daphne.paige.books

All rights reserved. No part of this book may be reproduced or used in any manner without written permission of the copyright owner except for brief quotations in a book review.

This is a work of fiction. Names, characters, places, and incidents are either the product of the author's imagination, or are used fictitiously. Any resemblance to actual events or persons, living or dead, is entirely coincidental.

To Necco. You and Nessie were my inspiration for book one. May you rest in peace with all the food and tubes you could want.

THE EMPIRE'S WITCH

⁜Pronunciation Page⁜

Ayne—(Ann)

Edelweiss—(Eh-dell-wise)

Maya—(My-ah)

Macellen—(Mah-kell-en)

Faramund—(Fair-ah-mund)

Rioghail—(Rye-og-hail)

Klymora—(Kly-more-ah)

Gaia—(Guy-ah)

Abhainn—(Ah-bay-n)

Cari—(Car-e)

Gardinzo—(Gar-deen-zo)

Nikolai—(Nick-oh-lie)

Caz—(Ca-az)

Bao—(Ba-ow)

Zhongguo—(Zhong-guo)

Lio—(Lee-oh)

CHAPTER ONE

The Apprentice

Sandalwood and myrrh burn around Maya. Her calm voice fills the air as she sings a melody that was once popular in Zhongguo, but now is forgotten by most. Bao hangs from a purple silk curtain framing the mirror above the dresser in front of Maya, nibbling on a portion of dried pear.

Bao is a vervet monkey, tufts of light brown fur surround his face and his eyes are as black as coal. The rest of his body is streaked with dark brown and white.

Maya stops singing to stroke Bao's face. "We have

guests arriving today," she says—her voice like a breeze, demanding no attention. The result of years of living in the shadows of Zhongguo. Sure, she's the only known witch—but witches aren't normally sought out.

She moves her hand away from Bao's warm face to remove a scroll from the top drawer of the dresser. She rereads King Ren's letter, announcing in intricate penmanship that he's sending his eldest daughter, Ayne, to apprentice under her.

"An apprentice," Maya whispers to Bao. "We haven't had an apprentice in this home for years."

Bao chatters in reply, dropping with a *thud* onto the surface of the dresser. A silver canister full of quills tips over, spilling the majority of the quills onto the floor. Bao snatches one that teeters on the edge, gripping the gray and white feather between his strong fingers. He presses the recently dipped end to his lips, leaving a smudge of blue ink.

Maya sighs, stooping to pick up the quills. "You're very messy, Bao," she chides, dropping the quills back into the canister after setting it upright. Footsteps grow louder outside—not everyday foot traffic passing on the main drag, like she thought at first, but intentional—*searching.*

She tilts her head slightly as her door—not usually locked during the day since she's almost always home—creaks open. A small hand protrudes from the red and purple beaded curtain blocking the entryway off from her living quarters. It's tan in pigment, and very feminine.

Maya groans as her shoulder-length black hair falls in front of her eyes. She shoves the tricky strands behind her ears and looks back up to find three pairs of eyes watching her. She can't hide her surprised expression—mouth fallen slightly open; eyes larger than normal.

She ignores Bao as he screeches again, demanding to know who these intruders are.

"I'm assuming one of you is Ayne?" Maya asks, studying the three figures that stand before her.

A girl with tan skin and long dark hair smiles, raising her hand—the same hand that pushed the curtain open—and gives a small wave. She can tell the girl has royal training by the way she holds herself. Strong and capable—but still, she is just a child.

"And who are they...?" Maya points to the other two. A taller man with blonde hair pulled into a high ponytail, a pale complexion, and inquisitive eyes. And a girl, definitely younger than Ayne, with a round face and a matching skin tone to the man.

"These are my friends. They wanted to come with me," Ayne says, introducing the man as Mason and the girl as Lio. "I hope that's not a problem. It was a last-minute decision."

Maya turns to look at Bao, raising an eyebrow in a silent question. Even though Bao doesn't know the Common language—it is still nice to turn to someone. "It's fine—a surprise, but not necessarily an unwelcome one. Please, come inside."

As the trio shuffles further into the living quarters, Maya lifts the scroll she was rereading to the candle beside her. It ignites in a puff of smoke and pink magic, filling the room with an even stronger scent of sandalwood.

She turns back around, narrowing her eyes at the awe on each of her guests' faces. Why are they in awe? Are they not aware that she is a witch? Magic is to be expected. The corners of her lips tug into a small smile and she waves the lingering pink smoke away. "When you're as skilled as me, you can do just about anything at any given time. Of course, smoke isn't the most impressive use of magic."

Ayne shakes her head, her long hair curtaining her back. She's wearing a beautiful orange dress that hangs loosely around her ankles, white and yellow flowers are embroidered around the hem. Her feet are decked in matching sandals, exposing her toes to the slight chill that seems constant in Maya's house.

The group's bags sit on the floor beside them—not much for how long they'll be staying.

"That's amazing…" Ayne exclaims, looking at her friends. She turns her attention back to Maya. "I heard that you were skilled—but can you really call on your magic at any time, to do *anything*?"

Maya just smiles in response. She starts walking toward the other side of the living quarters, her long blue dress sweeping behind her. "If you're wondering where you're all going to sleep, then follow me," she instructs. She leads them around a corner and down a small hallway with only two doors. She explains that one goes to the only lavatory in the house, and the other goes to their sleeping quarters. She pushes open the light brown door leading to the sleeping quarters and steps aside, letting her guests get a better view. A pair of beds are pushed against the far wall, laden with silky white sheets and soft blankets. A singular pillow rests on the bed to the right.

"I wasn't prepared for more than one person. Another pillow is in the closet over there," she nods to a closet beside the beds. The only other items in the room are a desk across from the beds, a wooden chair, and a worn burgundy rug. "One of you can sleep on the couch in the living quarters. I'll go set that up now."

"That'd be very nice, thank you," Mason agrees, scanning the small room. The only light is coming from a cluster of candles on the desk, which makes the shadows move on the wall as the flames flicker. "I'll let the ladies share this one. I wouldn't want to intrude on their privacy." He scratches the back of his neck, where his dirty hair tickles him. "I can help you arrange my spot in the other room if you want?"

Maya looks him up and down, furtively. She doesn't mind the companionship of two girls, but the last time a man resided in her home was…a very long time ago.

Without breathing a word, she moves past him, back into the living quarters. A bright red couch faces the fireplace in the center of the room, a knitted wool blanket is draped across the back of the couch and a throw pillow is squished into the corner crevice. Bao sits on the back of the couch, dissecting another pear he retrieved from the kitchen in a very messy manner.

"Bao," Maya calls, thrusting her hand toward the fireplace and igniting the kindling with a small flame—the same color pink as earlier. "Bring some of the lamb from the kitchen. We should get some food in our guests' stomachs." She glances back at Mason, who followed her into the main room. Any amusement that was once there drains from her. She turns to watch the flames lick across the wood. "You are hungry, are you not?"

Mason flushes, stumbling over his words. "Yeah. Starving actually. They didn't have much food on the boat. Just some beans and such... It wasn't very tasty either." He presses his lips into a line, the tip of his ears turning into a beacon with their brightness.

Her deep brown eyes linger on him. She can tell he hasn't eaten well. His stomach is thin and his skin is an unhealthy gray. "I showed you where the lavatory is at. Make use of it so you don't stink up the rest of my home." She waves a hand at him, crinkling her nose in a way meant to portray disgust... A question teases her mind: he seems too professional for such failed attempts at speaking, is that just her imagination?

Mason turns an even darker shade of red. He sputters, "Um, I'll go do that. Thank you."

Bao hops down from the couch and clambers to the kitchen, scowling at Mason as he passes. He comes back a few minutes later holding a brown parcel of fresh lamb and a handful of skewers. Maya bends down and pats him on the top of his head as he skewers the meat and starts cooking it over the flames.

Maya rests her hands on her hips as she watches her little monkey, the hairs on her neck stand on end and she looks over her shoulder. She furrows her brow. "Why are you still standing there staring at me?"

Mason fiddles with a strand of his hair and grins bashfully. "I—I don't know. I'll go."

With another glance toward Bao, she turns and leaves the room, casting a glare at Mason as she passes him. She calls over her shoulder, "Tell your friends that food is ready whenever they are." And, without waiting for a response, she walks down the second hallway branching directly off the kitchen and closes the door to her sleeping quarters.

Her room is illuminated by a red candle—almost completely melted. A dark canopy bed is cast in the eerie shadows that consume the farthest side. She likes it dark. It reminds her that she isn't welcome in the outside world, that she isn't normal... The darkness of her home reminds her of a cave—a place where she can be hidden away and do whatever she wants without judgment. She already receives enough of it when she goes out—a witch, and a lone woman. Women don't tend to live alone these days, finding it safer and more traditional to have a man with them.

She turns to face her dresser—the only other thing in the room, and on it is a painting of her and Nikolai, a dying bonsai tree in an orange ceramic pot, the candle, and a scrap of paper with a sentence sprawled in black ink...

I WILL SEE YOU AGAIN, MY LOVE. TRUST ME.

Maya kisses the print of her three fingers and rests it on the note. He promised he'd come back—but so far, no sign. It's been three years since he left and every day his connection to her feels weaker—but it's still there. She would know if he was dead.

Maya leans closer to the dresser, blowing out the

candle. It gives a final flicker before welcoming the darkness. She can see the white sheet wrapped above Nikolai's painting. She pulls the string holding it up, letting the sheet unravel to cover the painting—a perfect rectangle. Maya always does this when she's not going to be in the room for a while, to keep the dust from settling on his portrait.

A sigh escapes her lips, her hair falling around her face again. She pushes it back, sucking in a confident breath; she has so many plans today, so many lessons in store for her apprentice. She can't let the sorrow of Nikolai's absence take over—not again, and definitely not today.

A gentle knock sounds about her room and she looks up, startled. It'll definitely take some getting used to, but having guests in her home after so long might be nice. It'll draw her out more—save her from herself. She can't be a recluse forever.

Maya opens the door and peers out at the knocker. She suppresses a groan. "I see you've cleaned yourself. Good. Lunch should be done. Did you tell the girls?" she asks, stepping past Mason and closing the door before he can study her sleeping quarters. He may be staying here—and he may be a friend of the princess—

but that doesn't mean he has to know all her secrets, that he has to be *her* friend.

Mason runs his hands through his wet hair, his white long-sleeve tunic sticking to his chest. He winces, offering her a faint nod. "Yes, I made them aware. They should be in there now, eating."

Maya ignores him, walking into the living quarters to see for herself. Lio and Ayne are sitting on the floor in front of the fire, nibbling on a skewer of lamb. Lio's face is messy with grease, but she doesn't attempt to wipe it off.

Bao returned to his place on the back of the couch. He's watching the girls with a look of curiosity.

Maya clears her throat, raising an eyebrow as Bao turns his attention toward her instead. "Grab the guests some towels, won't you?" As Bao jumps down to go grab the towels from the kitchen, Maya's eyes drift over to the girls. "Enjoying your food?"

Lio grins broadly, nodding quickly. "Yes! The meat is so juicy and tasty. It's been a really long time since I've had such delicious lamb."

Maya smiles faintly. "Bao is an excellent cook."

"How'd you train a monkey to cook?" Ayne asks, staring at Bao with a new set of eyes. Her face is tinted with astonishment.

Maya lowers herself onto the couch, crossing her legs and resting her hands on her knees. Everybody's eyes are trained on her. She takes a steadying breath, trying to ignore the urge to get up and hide. "Monkeys are incredibly smart creatures. They rival the intelligence of humans."

She turns to face Bao, who has just wandered back into the living quarters, dropping a towel in front of Lio, and motioning for her to clean her face. Maya waves Bao over, clasping his hand in between her fingers. "It isn't hard, really. Bao was so desperate for love and acceptance when Nik—" she swallows his name, fending off threatening tears. She hasn't said his name aloud for quite some time. She composes herself, flashing an extra wide smile and continues, "when *I* found him. He does anything I tell him to."

"That's so cool!" Lio exclaims, patting Ayne on the shoulder. "Ayne has a pet just like that—except he's a gerbil."

Maya sits back, pinning Ayne with a questioning stare. "Is that so? And did you bring him along?"

Ayne brushes aside her long hair—now, Maya realizes, was used as a curtain to hide a small ball of white. "His name is Caz," Ayne says, smiling fondly at the little guy.

Maya inclines forward. Something dark swims in Ayne's eyes. She glances quickly away from Caz, dropping her hair to curtain him again.

Ayne offers the group an unsure smile—something clearly is plaguing her mind. Maya taps her bright pink fingernails against her knees.

"How old is your little friend?" Maya asks, getting closer to the subject she believes is upsetting Ayne.

Ayne visibly deflates. "Old. Let me just say that." She doesn't meet Maya's eyes, staring intently at the floor instead—then the fire, then the drawn crimson curtains behind Maya.

"I see," Maya mutters, helping Bao onto the couch. He cuddles against her side. "Bao is one. But he's been alive for three years." Her eyes glint mischievously, wondering if Ayne understands what she's implying.

Ayne scrunches her face—steam basically rising from her skull as she processes Maya's claim. "But that doesn't make sense..." Suddenly, as if she were struck by lightning, her eyes widen and she jumps up. She stares down at Maya, shaking her head. "Is that possible?"

Maya grins, reclining in her seat. "I'll show you, Ayne, and soon you'll begin to believe that anything is possible." Maya caresses Bao's cheek before planting a kiss on the bridge between his eyes. "I love you, my son."

Bao presses his face into her neck and wraps her in a hug.

"That is how he tells me he loves me too," Maya explains, running a hand down Bao's back lovingly. Her eyes flit to study Ayne's friends, an eyebrow raising on its own accord. "By the faces of your friends, they do not understand." Maya lingers on Mason's face, brow furrowed, biting lightly on his bottom lip, looking up to the ceiling as if the answer is falling toward him. Then his eyes lower to Maya, slowly, glistening with awe. Lio, on the other hand, looks completely confused. She's staring between Maya and Ayne, shrugging her shoulders animatedly. "Do they know why you're here?"

Ayne shrinks, blushing. "I—I couldn't find the right way to tell them."

Maya chuckles, finding this situation completely stupid, yet somehow endearing. Ayne's a witch, and yet she brought along people who don't even know? Does Ayne think they'll run from her, and come back at night with pitchforks? Witches are appreciated for their skill. Sure, some people would like to stab at them with farming utensils— but witches are still needed in this world, just in case there's a dire situation that needs a magical hand. "You do know what I am, right?" A smirk pulls at her lips.

"A witch," Lio says, nodding. "I saw you do magic when we came in. But, Ayne, why are we staying with a witch? No offense." She glances unsurely at her friend, both her dark eyebrows retreating into her hairline.

Maya smiles and waves her concern away. She's, surprisingly, finding enjoyment in this new revelation. "Shall I tell them, or should you, Ayne?"

Ayne gulps, running her palms down the sides of her dress. She looks to each of her friends and sighs. "I'll tell them. It'll probably be better coming from me."

Maya nods, waving for her to continue. Her rose-red smirk now full force. For some reason, she can't let it drop, even though her face muscles are begging to rest.

Mason, eagerly bouncing on the balls of his feet, whips his head around to look at Ayne. "What is it, Ayne?" he asks—hesitantly, as if trying a new exotic food on the tip of his tongue. It doesn't take much guess work for Maya to figure out that he's still not used to calling her Ayne, dropping her royal title completely.

Ayne begins, her voice quivers slightly, "The reason I'm here is because I'm apprenticing under Maya…"

"Apprenticing? For what?" Lio asks, tilting her head at the girl sitting next to her.

Mason grins…a grin full of beautiful pearl teeth. Maya quickly glances away, why did she notice a thing like that? *It doesn't matter,* she internally screams.

"I knew it!" he exclaims, beaming. "That's a unique blessing, Ayne. Congratulations."

Ayne seems shocked. Even Maya is taken aback… He considers witchcraft a blessing?

"I'm not sure if it's a blessing," Ayne says, shaking her head glumly. She takes a deep breath and then lifts her hand in front of her face, showing everyone the faint haze of purple that outlines it. "I'm a witch," she adds for Lio, who still hasn't caught on. "And I need to learn how to control it."

CHAPTER TWO

The Blessing

Lio rocks in her seat underneath a sun-faded umbrella in Maya's backyard. Her eyes are frozen on a spot in the center of the wooden table.

Bao climbs onto the table, holding a cup of freshly squeezed lemonade from the lemon tree in the corner of the yard. It splashes against the rim as he shoves it toward Lio, insisting she takes it with a high-pitched screech.

Maya shuts the door behind her and makes her way across the small yard, pulling out the chair beside

Lio. "Did you not suspect Ayne of being a witch at all, Lio?" she asks, cutting to the real reason she came outside. The sun and her don't mix.

"That my queen is a witch? No. Not at all. The thought never even crossed my mind," she admits, her voice quiet...shaken. She shakes her head and takes a long drink from the glass of lemonade in front of her, downing half the glass.

"Your queen? You do know that Ayne still has five years before she's crowned in Gaia?" Maya asks, resting her elbows on the table and leaning toward Lio, her chin propped in the hammock of her hands.

Lio looks at her quizzically. "Yeah, I know she's not the queen yet—but she will be. But, do *you* know that Ayne isn't going to be the queen of Gaia?"

Maya raises her eyebrows. "But she is the princess..."

Lio nods in an *I-know-it's-so-confusing* kind of way. "But she's marrying Prince Talin of Klymora. So, she's going to be the queen of Klymora in five years instead. I think her sister, Kaiva, is going to take over Gaia."

Maya shares a look with Bao. How come nobody in Zhongguo heard of this? It's a huge deal, especially since it involves the neighboring royalty. It must be a very recent decision... Maya chews on her thoughts carefully—her eyes flitting around the yard. She lands on Ayne, watching her as she laughs with Mason. She's so young...and engaged to be married? Maya shakes her head, never understanding why people marry at such a young age—of course, she isn't a royal, so maybe she will never understand.

Without a single thought, she's switched from watching Ayne to staring at her own hands. The silver band around her ring finger, a small water drop engraved on the underside, glints in the sunlight.

She doesn't even realize Lio is speaking until her soft fingers graze her arm. "Were you listening? I was telling you why Ayne is my queen even though she hasn't been crowned yet."

Maya drops her hands to her lap, hiding the ring from sight. Her curiosity surges back up, wondering what the answer to her original question is. "Sorry. Go on."

Lio smiles, continuing on as if nothing even happened—as if Maya's heart isn't crumbling inside her chest at the thought of the silver looped around her finger, at the thought of Nikolai.

"Ayne's appearance in Klymora was monumental,

she pushed for the freedom of slaves. I was brought into court after being found—I was taken from my family, and shoved into a carriage with five other girls. All around my age." She looks down into her glass, her cheery mood shifting to something darker—grizzlier. She shakes her head slightly, making her long brown hair bounce. "She made sure I didn't go back to that life. She freed me. Without her, I doubt I would've been saved," she finishes, her voice cracking. She clears her throat and looks back up at Maya. Her eyes glisten with unshed tears.

Maya finds herself at a loss of words. Ayne, a child, did that much? She *saved* people? But what happened to Lio and the five other girls? What dampened her mood so quickly? A single idea pops into her mind—so revolting that she refuses it as even a possibility. But it lingers against her will...connecting dots that she doesn't want to see. Anger sloshes in her stomach, and her blood turns to ice. *Fine,* she screams inside her head. *You may be right.*

When Maya's eyes meet Lio's, she can tell that her persistent mind is, in fact, correct. That all those horrible scenarios that kept blooming to life, taking place in her brain forevermore, may have actually happened. And that sickens her.

She furrows her brow, digging her nails into the palms of her hands so she doesn't punch something—Nikolai always told her that her anger is uncontrollable, that it's fueled by her magic, believing that it should be in charge—that everything should happen the way *it* desires. Nikolai said that his magic does the same too, that it's a curse all witches and sorcerers have to deal with. It lessens as the witch or sorcerer learns to make their magic obey *them*—but it's always there. Magic always wants to be the one in charge.

"Klymora, what a messed-up place," Maya growls, pushing a simple breeze spell from her fingertips to try to cool herself off.

"Is Zhongguo any better?" Lio asks, arching an eyebrow.

Maya sighs, feeling the red-hot burn of her anger diminish. "I don't know. I don't get out much. But what I do know is that Gaia and Zhongguo would never allow its citizens to be enslaved."

Lio smiles sadly, casting her eyes back to the table. "Gaia has warriors watch the capitol, but I don't think the Edelweiss family pays much attention to the other cities."

Maya looks back over at Ayne, who's brought a chair from inside to sit down on, leaving Mason to sit in the grass. Maya's lips twist into a smile: *the princess doesn't want to dirty her dress.* "I see," she says. "I suppose people must have their priorities."

"Yeah. I just hope they post more warriors in the other cities; I fear what happened to me will happen to another unsuspecting girl." Lio finishes her lemonade and scoots the glass to the center of the table. "I'm thinking of moving to Gaia permanently when we get back. I know I'd feel much safer."

"That would be a wise decision, I'm sure Ayne would help you settle in," Maya adds with a small nod.

Lio beams. "I know she would! She's a great friend!"

Maya stands abruptly from the table, having received the answer she came outside originally to get. She glances back down at Lio's surprised expression, realizing that her socializing skills are a lot rustier than she thought. *I guess one does excuse themselves from a conversation,* she says mentally, chiding herself for her rudeness.

She smiles politely at Lio. "I do apologize. It's

about time Ayne and I start our first lesson. Would you like to watch?"

Lio jumps from her seat, grinning like a child on their birthday. "Yes! That would be amazing!"

"What's amazing?" Ayne calls from her chair, peering over at the two at the table, her head cocked. Caz rests in her lap.

"I get to watch you perform witchcraft!" Lio shouts, scaring a bird from the lemon tree. It caws and darts into the sky, flapping its black wings to get away from the commotion as quickly as possible.

Maya winces, gesturing for Lio to stay silent. "You don't want the whole neighborhood to know Ayne is a witch."

"Oops," Lio giggles sheepishly. "Sorry!"

Ayne makes her way toward them, Mason following quickly behind. "Is it really time for my first lesson?" She pawns Caz off onto her shoulder, pulling her hair up and twisting it into a messy bun, using her own hair as a sort of tie.

"It is, indeed," Maya responds, grabbing Bao's hand. She leads the group back inside, relishing the return of the darkness. "Please, make your way into the living quarters." She watches her guests file into the room before detouring to the kitchen. She swipes a pair of lemons off the counter, handing one to Bao who accepts it happily. He squeezes it between his hands, the acidic juice drips down his arm, matting his hair. He crams the pulp into his mouth—squished peel and all.

Maya kisses him on the head. "A taste of home, my son," she whispers, toying with a few long strands of his white hair.

When she returns to the living quarters, she finds Ayne sitting properly on the couch, her ankles crossed. Caz is sitting on her lap, peering at the people around them.

Mason is sitting on the other side of the couch, studying the room and all its décor. And Lio is sitting on the floor in front of the still-lit fireplace, her eyes shining with excitement. She's bouncing up and down with pent-up energy.

Maya releases Bao's hand. He lumbers over to the mantle and scales the side, sitting among various unlit candles and long-since-dead flowers to watch over the group.

Maya kneels next to Lio, her features growing serious as she switches to mentor mode. "Shall we begin?"

Ayne nods curtly. "What are we learning today?"

"Do you remember earlier, how I implied that Bao doesn't age?"

Ayne nods again. "Yeah... That's really fascinating. How did you do that? Does it make him live for eternity?" She sits up a little straighter. "Does it make him invincible if someone...tried to hurt him?"

Maya shakes her head. "I will answer all those questions in due time. But first, I need to begin the lesson."

Ayne blushes. "Sorry—please continue."

"It's fine. As I was saying, our lesson for today is the age spell, the same one I used on Bao years ago." She holds out her palm. "May I see Caz?"

Ayne seems weary as she scoops Caz up and sets the now-very-alert gerbil onto Maya's outstretched hand. Caz looks up at Maya with curious eyes. Maya smiles gently at the small creature, sweeping her finger down his back; magic begins to envelop him.

"Is that it? Are you done?" Ayne asks, reaching over to take Caz back. Her brow is tightly knitted, creating a line of worry across her forehead.

"Not yet. That was to calm him down, to make

him see that I'm not going to hurt him..." Maya purses her lips; the energy around Caz seemed slightly off. Her magic doesn't read the energy around people as strongly as others. Her magic excels more at changing things, transforming them, but she could still sense his unease...

Maya can't help but wonder why is he so uneasy... Is he used to being afraid of people? Or, is there someone specific he's afraid of?

"Are there any possibilities that this won't work?" Ayne asks, nibbling on her bottom lip. "Could this hurt him?"

Maya sighs. "There is always a possibility. The only thing you can do is believe it'll work."

Ayne forces a smile. "Oh. Okay." Her voice doesn't sound reassured.

Maya holds Caz in one hand and in the other she holds the lemon she retrieved. Her words are quiet, floating from her mouth like the lyrics of a song. Pink magic swirls around her, lifting her hair up and setting it back on her shoulders. Her skin glows, youthfully, and any blemishes on her skin disappear. When she looks around the room, she can tell the others are reaping the rewards of her magic; those in close proximity usually do.

Caz squeaks excitedly. And then...the magic stops, and he slumps over in her hand. The lemon slowly deflates, dripping juice down Maya's arm and onto the floor. Maya watches the juice drip, then her gaze swings over to the rodent's small body. Still and silent. A hand of fear grabs her heart—even though she knows she shouldn't be afraid, that there is nothing to be afraid of. Still, however, the constant thought echoing in the back of her mind haunts her: *what if you aren't good enough? What if you screwed up? What if everything is your fault?*

"What happened? Is he...?" Ayne shouts, tears pricking her eyes. "No, no!" She crumbles in on herself, shaking as tears flood from her eyes uncontrollably.

Maya tilts her head at the small creature's lifeless body. "Do not worry. This always happens." She brings Caz up to her mouth and blows gently, sending a puff of magic to surround him. It courses through the gerbil's body, bringing him back to life—except, he's different. He doesn't have the body of an elderly gerbil anymore, he's young...maybe one or two. He chirps and his fuzzy lips tug into a smile. The echoes in her mind dim until they're securely planted in the background, exactly where they belong.

Ayne's eyes widen and her mouth hangs open. "What? How?" A tear continues to trace a trail down her cheek.

Maya chuckles. "It is advanced witchcraft. It's my gift to you." She lets Caz climb off her hand and back onto Ayne's lap. He wiggles his tail, quite content.

Ayne scoops him up excitedly, studying her companion. His ears perk up at her and he thumps his feet wildly in her palm. Ayne's eyes flicker with something close to admiration as she stares at Maya. "Can you teach me how to do that?"

Maya smiles; a very small smile. "You've been my apprentice for less than a day. You can't control your powers any better than a baby witch-born. This is a challenging spell to learn, so no. Not yet."

"Then how was that a lesson if I'm not learning anything myself?" Ayne asks.

Maya chuckles, "You've learned how powerful magic can be. Now, after seeing that, I'm sure you can believe in anything." As she looks at Ayne, a new emotion darts across her face: *pride*. "I do like that you're curious. Reminds me of someone I know." And then her expression falters, creasing her face with a frown. She looks toward the window, squinting as if she can see past the drawn crimson curtains...wishing that he's walking up to the door right now; that he's finally coming back after so long away.

CHAPTER THREE

The Painting

Maya traces the rough curves of Nikolai's jaw, then trails her fingertips down the center of his brow, right between his bright blue eyes...

He's different from everybody here. He isn't of Zhongguonese descent—fair skin, big brown eyes, and naturally curvy bodies. He's as pale as a white lamb, with dark brown stubble spread across his square chin, a crooked smile that always makes her heart skip a beat, and a previously broken nose—leaving it knotted in the center.

She looks at herself in the painting. Her head rested on her husband's shoulder, a childish grin stretching across her face, and their right hands intertwined, showing their matching silver rings. On the inside of his is a small flame, symbolic of Maya.

A tear drips down Maya's cheek and she sniffles, drawing it from her face to linger in the air, inches above her fingers. A faint pink haze bounces off its reflective surface; water and fire... That's what she was with Nikolai. He was the water to extinguish her flames. He always put her in the best mood—an eternity of happiness, that's what he promised her. And she believed him. She starts to cry, allowing the sorrow that boiled inside her the entire day, growing and growing like water against a dam, to finally release. She knows that the saddest part is she still believes him—she still believes in their happiness.

Maya's heart bursts with warmth and she doubles over, clutching at her sides as she staggers backward onto her bed, sinking into the shadows that inhabit her sleeping quarters.

Maybe he can sense her misery—maybe he can feel the weight of each teardrop as it leaves her eyes.

Maybe then he'll come back.

Ayne peers up from the list in her hand, scanning the market stalls around them. Maya can see the curious etch of her apprentice's brows and she sighs, stopping her in the middle of the busy street. It's been a while since she's been outside—around people—and she finds that she doesn't know quite what to do. She pondered on that thought on the walk over, having come to the conclusion that it can't be nearly as bad as hanging out around normal people—people who are completely accepted by society. This particular market deals with those who live in the shadows, the mavericks.

"What are you thinking?" Maya asks calmly, tilting her head at the younger girl.

Ayne shifts on her feet, lifting her chin higher to meet Maya's eyes—well, she *tries* to meet her eyes. But she glances away after a short amount of time passes. "I don't know this place. I don't know what all these ingredients are, and I don't know what the potion we're going to make will do." She looks at the parchment in her hand and takes a deep breath. "Can't you tell me?"

Maya puckers her lips as she thinks. She recalls Nikolai saying that curiosity is a burden that many people have to bear, and its weight is heavy. So, she decides to lift that burden from the young witch. She decided originally not to tell her to see what she would do, but now, after seeing the eagerness in her eyes, she couldn't hold out any longer. But, even with the faint thought of Nikolai, images of her outburst earlier flood through her mind… She can't help but think of how foolish she is. She grimaces, shaking the thoughts from her head. *Focus,* she scolds, *now is not the time.*

"It's a simple spell, really. Transformation. The only difficulty is reserving your energy, storing it up to use when the time arrives, and then concentrating on your subject for the duration of the spell." She scans for a particular stall through the sea of patrons. A smile spreads across her lips as she lands on her target. An older woman with long gray dreadlocks held away from her forehead by an orange scarf is tending to a line of customers.

"That doesn't sound simple…" Ayne replies,

scrunching her face. "Have you ever done it before?" She blinks, staring up at her mentor.

Maya sighs at such a silly question. "Would I teach someone something I do not know myself?" She shakes her head. "I have turned a rat into a dog. A squirrel into a cat. A goat into a horse. And...a monkey into a man." Her eyes cast downward and she shrugs a thought away—she will not think of him now, nor of their past.

Ayne seems to notice her mentor's downcast expression and asks, "What's wrong?"

Maya waves her away, deciding to go with a truth—just not the truth she was thinking of. "My only flaw was that I could never turn them back into what they were. I was left with a dog. A cat. A horse." She tries to find the same volume to finish her list, but her throat refuses to behave, not when it's choked by emotions. She sighs and says with a cracked voice, "And a man."

"A man?" Ayne mutters, then her eyes widen. "Your love?"

Maya turns her face away from the inquisitive princess. Startled by how quickly she caught on—is it really that noticeable? "Maybe. Who knows now? Who knows if he'll ever come back? If he's created a new life in Rutheria, with a new girl on his arm...maybe he stepped back into his old life and left me behind." Her lip trembles and she blinks away the water balancing on her thick eyelashes. Why did she say that? Any of that? Her burdens aren't Ayne's...

"I think he'll come back," Ayne whispers, fidgeting nervously with the long sweeping sleeves of her new dress; Maya gave her an unworn dress she had stashed in the back of her armoire. At least someone can get some use from it. It's a brilliant blue with a sash the color of blood.

Ayne's words raise the hairs on Maya's arm as if the princess can sense Maya's own thoughts, as traitorous as they may be. *I think he'll come back*...is the exact phrase echoing underneath all her memories and thoughts...a constant voice telling her to not lose hope. But it's a small voice and is constantly drowned out by her common sense. By logic. If he was going to come back, wouldn't he have already?

"Maybe," Maya finally says. She dusts her own dress off and composes herself, turning her attention back to the old woman tending the stall across the street. "Nevertheless, don't worry yourself with my life. Let's get the things we came here for and go home."

Ayne nods, following Maya to the stall; the woman has sat down at her desk in the very back, between racks of fur cloaks and bottled elixirs. Her eyes are pinched closed and her hands are splayed out over a set of cards.

"Lady Marinette," Maya exclaims, placing her hand on the desk. The woman flinches and looks up at her, a small smile curls her lips.

"Maya, good to see you again." Her eyes, one silver and one brown, turn to Ayne. She cocks her head, allowing her fingers to grasp at the air in front of the princess. "Hmm, an aura so pure. Unaffected. Who is she?" she asks, watching Maya again.

Maya offers the woman a smile, clearly tired of her old tricks, and nods toward a chest beside her desk. It's old and worn, the bronze latches are rusted and a string of distant words are scrawled across the front in gold paint. It's obvious she isn't going to answer the woman's question.

Lady Marinette collects her cards, sorts them, then sprawls them out on the desk again. She runs a hand over them before plucking the center one up. "The tower," she drawls, flipping it over so they can see the hazy blue rendition of a stone tower. "Things are changing, can't you feel it around you?"

Maya, so tempted to roll her eyes, ignores her, tapping her finger on the desk until she gains Lady Marinette's attention once again. "I have come for my package."

Lady Marinette scowls. "You're no fun, Maya. So serious all the time." She stands up from her desk, taking a key from the top drawer, then leans down and unlocks the chest. A few brown parcels are stacked together, notes are plastered on top of them declaring who they are for. She shuffles through them until she finds one meant for Maya. It's small, barely as big as Marinette's palm. "What did you order this time?"

"It's not for me," Maya states, tucking the package into her dress pocket—a custom addition. Dresses in Zhongguo aren't normally made with pockets—a huge mistake if the dress makers bothered to ask anyone. "We need to pick a few more things out. We have a list. Can you help us find them?"

Marinette smiles, looking over the list that Ayne puts forth, nodding appreciatively. "Ah, yes. Good. Good." She looks back up at the pair and grins. "Stay here, I'll be right back."

The older woman walks away from the table, stepping past customers and around shelves, grabbing vials and containers and parcels of dried meat. Marinette looks contently around the shop, checking to see if she missed anything, before coming back to the desk. She places the objects she's carrying with a satisfying *thunk* on the desk.

"Owl eye. Peppered squirrel. Cow's tongue. And one new ladle," she says, pointing to each item in turn. She swivels to view her display of fresh fruits, sitting in a wicker bowl on a worn side table behind her. "And finally, one banana." She places the fruit with the rest of their goods. "That'll be one secret, Maya." Her eyes sparkle with mischief as the words leave her lips.

Maya nods understandingly, leans in, and whispers, "This is my apprentice." She can't hide the cocky smile that slips onto her face.

Marinette glances at Ayne, scanning her up and down. She frowns. "Another witch? Oh, my. But I couldn't sense her…"

Maya shrugs, her smile growing larger. "One secret is all you required." She waits, tapping her foot repeatedly against the ground as Marinette places the items in a bag and slides it back across the desk.

"That is right, darling." Her mismatched eyes linger on Ayne, even as the next customer walks up to the desk.

As they join the stream of patrons wandering around the marketplace, Ayne turns to Maya and asks, "Is she a witch?" She dodges a child running by, holding a wooden Pegasus to the sky, then continues, "It's just, she seems...to know things. And what are the cards for?"

Maya lifts an eyebrow and chuckles. "No, she isn't a witch. She's a gypsy. Human-born and magicless. Gypsies are common here in Ziana. And the cards are tarot cards. It's said that your aura leads you to the card you're supposed to pick. Gypsies use their auras, unlike witches, who use their hearts. Their passion." Her hand clenches into a fist in front of her heart, signifying her words.

"Oh," Ayne mutters, nibbling carefully on her lip as she thinks, her eyes trained on Maya's fist. "Why is she called Marinette? That can't be her birth name, right?" Ayne moves her eyes upward until she's staring directly at Maya.

"So very full of questions, you are," Maya says

with a smile. She notices a chill drift across her skin... She shakes it off, and adds, "Keep asking them. And you're correct. She is called Marinette because she used to be the prettiest woman in Zhongguo. She could control any man alive, bending them to her will, playing with their heartstrings. She hasn't lost her beauty, but it *has* dimmed."

Ayne acknowledges her words, taking one last look at the woman—Lady Marinette. Maya follows her gaze, confirming her exact thoughts, that the chill that snaked down her body was from the woman's piercing eyes—the silver and brown that still follow them.

CHAPTER FOUR

The Spell

Maya bends over to stare into the eyes of a common thief—black, white, and gray. She clicks her tongue and chuckles. The raccoon is trapped in a bronze cage, shaded by the worn burgundy tent the *Live Animals* booth is located under. A price tag in front of it reads, in simple cursive: *400*.

Maya stands back up and turns to the man behind her—a thin, faux smile tempting his lips. Mister Gardinzo has never been a pleasure—yet he's the only one who sells live animals in Zaina.

"Find what you're looking for, *Maya*?" Gardinzo

drawls, his ring-covered hand cups his chin. A dark mustache is like a rodent sprawled across his upper lip.

"I have. I'll take this," she exclaims, pointing a finger at the raccoon. "Is it," she searches for the word, "aggressive?"

Gardinzo laughs humorlessly. "You can speak in Zhongguonese, Maya. I know it's the most comfortable for both our tongues." The small silver loops in his ears catch a fallen ray of sunshine, drifting in from the holey canopy—it's too bright and she looks away.

Switching to her native language, she sighs. The words are sweet and melodic—much better than the Common tongue—a language most everybody is nearly fluent in. "Yes, I guess I can, *Gardinzo*." She watches him from the corner of her eye as she inspects the creature again. "Can I take it in the cage?"

"Were you planning to stick it in your pocket?" Gardinzo jeers, a real smile finally finding way. "Take the cage. That'll be four hundred."

Maya nods approvingly, then looks over at her apprentice—who's inspecting a stall across the lane. Ayne's finding a souvenir for her sister is what Maya was told.

She turns back to Gardinzo and digs the coins from

her pocket. The gold gleams in the single ray. Gardinzo puts them into the bag slung around his waist and grins.

Maya shudders—a Gardinzo grin is the most unsettling thing.

"What did you find for your sister?" Maya asks, breaking the awkward silence between her and Ayne on their walk through the market and back towards her home in the center of Zaina city.

Ayne beams up at her, clearly thankful to be rid of the oppressing quiet. "Kaiva has always loved Caz—and she's been wanting to get piercings—even though I've told her it is completely un-princess like…" She shakes her head and opens her hands, showing a pair of small clay gerbil earrings. The gerbils are brown with black beady eyes. "I think she'll love them."

Maya's lips turn up at the edges as she peels her eyes away from the earrings and back to the walkway. "I think so too."

Ayne lowers her eyes to the cage gripped in Maya's far hand, cloaked by a black blanket. The smile on her face fades. "What is that?" She irks an eyebrow.

Maya shifts the cage away from her student. Her big brown eyes glisten with mystery. "You'll find out soon enough. Please don't worry."

Ayne looks like she's about to say something—but she presses her lips together and sighs. "Fine."

Maya pushes open the door to her home; a small house built along the main road with a dark alley on both sides—and large community tenements built beside those. Across the street is a run-down market, selling low-quality—but cheap—goods. Nothing like the wares sold at the market Maya and Ayne visited.

The living quarters are dark and empty. Maya's eyes scan the room, searching for any sign of her new guests. "Did your friends say what they were going to do?"

Standing on her tippy-toes Ayne peers into the

room from behind her. "No. I just told them you were taking me to the market to buy items for our lesson today."

"Hmm," Maya mumbles, stepping across the threshold. Her house seems different... She sets the cage down by the doorway.

They walk through the living quarters and past the kitchen, down the small hallway, and to the left. Her sleeping quarter's door is shut, exactly as she left it. And the lavatory door down the next hall is closed as well. The door leading to the backyard is left open a crack and the chilly late-summer breeze drifts across their skin.

A sound Maya isn't accustomed to trails from the outside—a loud, beautiful sound.

"Is that...laughter?" Maya asks. She pushes the door open further, her eyes widening at the scene unfolding in front of her.

Bao hangs from the lemon tree in the corner, making distinct screeching noises. Lio and Mason are sitting in the grass, their backs to the house, laughing as Bao performs: plucking unripe lemons from the tree and eating them, contorting his face; scratching his armpits; mimicking Caz, who sits on Lio's shoulder, tilting his little head in confusion at the strange sounds coming from the monkey.

Ayne chuckles beside Maya, stealing the duo's attention. Bao stops, a smile still on his face. Caz thumps his feet excitedly when he sees Ayne, begging to be reunited. Mason stands and dusts off his trousers, which are now stained by the grass. He smiles sheepishly at Ayne and drops to a half-bow. "I'm sorry, Your Highness, your courtier shouldn't be acting so…" He struggles to find the right word, scrunching his face in the process.

Lio swats a hand at him and snickers. "Ayne doesn't care, Mason! I mean, maybe she used to…but now, she's changed." Something sparkles in her eyes—something accusing and knowing.

Maya watches her apprentice…she knows that look. That's the look of love…so a boy changed the princess of Gaia? What was she like beforehand?

Ayne smiles at her friends. "It's perfectly alright Sir Mason. Lio is right—this is a vacation of sorts. I'm not princess here, so I think it'll be fine if we all let our hair down." To signify her words, she sweeps her hand through her hair; small threads of gold fall to the floor. She gestures to Bao. "Please, continue. Caz and I would love to watch the show." The smile that tugs her lips is genuine and kind.

Maya nods to Bao when he looks over at her, tilting his head to ask for permission. "Shall we take a seat, then?" She pulls out the chairs by the table and sits down, crossing her legs and resting a hand on her knee. Ayne sits beside her.

Bao's chatter is loud, resounding through the yard as he jumps from tree branch to tree branch.

Ayne turns to face Maya, excitement, and curiosity plastered on her small face. "Are we going to do the transformation lesson today?"

Maya shakes her head, not taking her eyes away from her companion. "Tomorrow. Today, let's just have fun."

CHAPTER FIVE

The Transformation

Maya walks into the living quarters with Mason. His blonde hair hangs loosely around his shoulders and a slight smile plays on his lips. His blue eyes wander to Maya, trailing a short strand of pesky hair that insists on tickling her cheeks. Then those beautiful eyes meet Maya's, lingering longer than most would be comfortable with.

Maya looks away first, clearing her throat. She grabs the blanket off the back of the couch and spreads it out, pushing it into the corners to make it smooth.

She pulls the pillow out from the corner of the couch and attempts to fluff it up, letting it lean against the armrest. She turns back around, gesturing to the makeshift bed. "Here you go," Maya says, frowning as he continues to stare at her. Did he even hear her words? "Mason. You'll be sleeping here."

Mason seems to fall out of a daze. He rests his hand on the back of his neck and looks down at the couch. "I—uh, thanks."

Maya narrows her eyes at him. But she can't get lost in thought now—*not now*. She can't think about how his blue eyes remind her of Nikolai's. She can't take into account the blush on his cheeks or the nervous set of his mouth. She forces herself to shrug, to be done with this interaction. "It's not a problem. Please, have a good night."

Maya hurries back to the guests' quarters. She can feel Mason's eyes lingering on her until she's completely out of view. She rests her hand on the doorframe and leans into the room; Lio is sitting cross-legged on the left bed, peering over at Ayne, who's brushing her hair. Their bags are sitting on the floor in the middle of the room.

"Oh, hi!" Lio exclaims, waving excitedly when she

spots Maya. Lio is dressed in a long white nightgown; ruffles cuff the bottom of her skirt and around her collar.

Ayne glances up at Maya, setting the brush on the dresser. "Hello, Maya. Thank you for the place to stay." Caz, who is laying on Ayne's shoulder beneath her smooth waves, grins up at Maya. The best grin a tiny rodent can muster.

Maya smiles at the children. "Of course. Your father wouldn't have it any other way." She pauses, rethinking her words. *Did that sound harsh, by chance?* She tries again: "Anything for my apprentice."

"Do you really mean that?" Ayne asks, raising an eyebrow, oblivious to Maya's inner dialogue.

Maya bats her eyelashes, an attempt at innocence, and crosses her arms. "Yes, I do." She really hopes her words sound genuine. "Sleep well."

Ayne wipes her greasy fingers on a handkerchief, then dabs the grease from her lips. Maya and Bao prepared an excellent duck for lunch—so excellent that Ayne had more than a princess probably should.

Mason and Lio are sitting next to her on the floor in the living quarters, the fireplace is lit—but somehow the flames are cold, perfect for the late summer.

Bao is sitting next to Maya on the couch, his furry arm draped around her and his head resting on her shoulder. His eyes are closed in slumber and his chest rises and drops peacefully.

"Today Ayne is going to do her first spell," she explains, resting the palms of her hands on her knees. "It is going to be challenging, since you've never drawn on your power before. But it'll be exciting and you'll learn a lot."

Ayne is trying to mask the excitement from her face, but fails at doing a good job. Her brown eyes are wide and her lips are drawn upward.

Maya stands up from the couch—ignoring Bao's sleepy grumbles. She grabs the cage by the entrance and sets it in the center of the living quarters, in front of the three observers. She lifts the blanket off, taking note of Ayne's expression; her question of what's in the cage is finally answered.

"A raccoon?" Ayne asks, tilting her head at the

creature. Her once wide eyes are now squinted.

The raccoon is looking wildly between the group; its eyes are almost black, and its light gray fur looks yellow in the sunlight filtering through the window drapes.

Maya nods, splaying her hands while she speaks. "I don't know what you draw on, but I use the darkness. For the rebirth of your friend," she gestures to Caz, "I used lemons—something fresh and lively, to rejuvenate him. It really depends on the spell. And on the witch."

Ayne's lips are pressed in a thin line and she nods. "Okay." She shares a look with Caz then turns to the raccoon in front of them. She lifts her hands, facing them toward the cage. The raccoon backs away from her, pressing itself against the bronze bars. It hisses, a low and scared sound. "Do I just—?" Purple magic seeps from her fingertips; the tendrils swirl toward the cage, looping around it and dispersing through the bars.

The raccoon's hair stands on end as the magic licks across its body; panic seizes its features.

"Just like that," Maya whispers, leaning forward. She rests her chin in her hand in awe, her apprentice is catching on rather quickly.

"Now what?" Ayne shouts, as if the magic is deafening her.

"Think of what you want to turn it into," Maya says, with a single eyebrow lifted, concentrating on her apprentice as if she can give her enough power with a stern stare.

Ayne furrows her brow, pushing her hands closer to the caged animal. Her lips quiver with the strain.

Just as the purple magic disappears from the air, and her hands drop to the floor, the raccoon starts to shift. It's a painful image to watch. Its spine protrudes from its back, the silver and black fur slides off, then the skeletal creature shrinks. When its fur grows back, it's a light brown. A tail, thin and fluffy; eyes, big and bold; a face exactly like Caz's.

Ayne crawls closer to the cage, watching in bewilderment at the small rodent.

"You chose…to transform it into a gerbil?" Lio asks, cocking her head.

Ayne breaks into a grin. She's wheezing from exertion as she says, "I did it! I really did it! I did magic."

Maya picks the cage up and holds it out in front of

her. She narrows her eyes as she watches the rodent scamper around the cage. Her apprentice did extraordinarily well, the only other person who wielded such power without much training was Nikolai. "You did, indeed, my young apprentice." She clicks her tongue. "But this is just the beginning." She looks at Ayne from the corner of her eyes, appraisingly. There's talent beneath the soft exterior...something incredibly grand. Once all the dust common to beginners is blown away, a diamond will surely become visible.

"What spell is next?" Ayne asks, still staring at the gerbil. She shifts her eyes down to her hands—the grin never breaking from her face. "I still can't believe I did it. It seemed so impossible, so uncontrollable, when I was in Klymora. But here? It isn't too hard."

Maya places the cage back down and sets her jaw. "Don't get ahead of yourself. Magic is *very* hard. Do not underestimate it."

Ayne turns her attention to something beside her—not Caz, nor Lio or Mason. Something in the space between, something invisible to Maya's eyes.

Maya looks down at her fingers—the heat of her magic flickers across her skin and she recoils. Concern paints her face. Why is her magic flaring up? It's never done this before.

Ayne quickly ducks her head, whispering under her breath.

"What is it?" Maya asks—a little too urgently, she draws all their attention. She manages to compose herself before saying again, "What is it?"

Mason glances between the two girls, confusion marring his face.

Ayne shakes her head at Maya, lost for words until she finally mutters, "I—I can't say really." Her own hands are gloved in purple.

"Why not?" Maya presses—desperation lacing between each syllable, like poison swirling in wine. You wouldn't know it was really there unless you paid close attention.

This is when Ayne meets her eyes; an emotion close to fear and confusion swims in their brown depths. "I—I was told not to."

CHAPTER SIX

The Discovery

Maya runs a finger along the spines of old, weathered leather books. They're written by ancient witches and gypsies—all long gone. She stops and pulls out a book with beveled golden edges. The words which are also gold are scrolled across the inside cover in neat penmanship: *Those Who Whisper to None.*

Marinette hovers behind her—she knows this without looking because of the insistent smell of flowers and orange zest: Marinette's signature perfume.

"Ah, so you're looking for curses and such?" she whispers, leaning a little too close. She reads the first page over Maya's shoulder and sighs. "What odd research for *the* Maya Lee. The one who claims to know everything." She chuckles as if it's a little joke—not a petty stab at Maya herself.

Maya darts her eyes toward the woman and scowls. "Do you have any more books like this? Any that'll tell me why magic reacts to, seemingly, nothing?"

Marinette considers this for a moment, then she shrugs. With a quick scan of the bookshelf, pushing aside vials of floating frog entrails in a questionable liquid, she selects a thin red book and blows dust off the cover. She hands it over. "This is the best one—covers everything you're looking for."

Maya reads the title: *Secrets of Magic.*

She returns her gaze to the older woman and huffs, blowing a loose strand of her hair away from her cheek. *Why does it insist on pestering her at all the wrong times?* "I'll take them both."

Marinette claps her hands together, then leads her through the growing line of patrons to her desk. She sweeps aside her tarot cards and takes a seat in her chair. With her fingertips tented together and a mischievous smile stitched across her face, she says, "That'll cost you a secret. Just one." Her mismatched eyes twinkle—and it makes Maya wonder, for the hundredth time since knowing her—how she stays in business with just a currency of words.

"To answer your prior question: yes, my apprentice, Ayne, is a witch," she says, in such a low voice that Marinette has to strain to hear.

The older woman's eyes grow large and a small cackle leaves her throat. "I knew it! But who is Ayne...with a skin tone like that...with beautiful wide eyes...with such delicate hands?" She clucks and leans back in her chair, crossing her age-speckled arms. "Almost, dare I say, like a royal." She presses her lips together, and fans out her cards, humming a tune that's short and menacing—very close to ancient Zhongguonese battle songs. "I'm going to read for you." Marionette runs her hand above her cards and draws one smack in the middle. When she flips it over, a smile stretches her lips—a sort of knowing, aware, smile. "The Lovers," she announces, setting it in front of Maya. "I'm sure you can interpret that."

Maya chews on her bottom lip—a habit derived from nervousness, but she's never considered herself to be a nervous person—just an unkind jumble of other things: socially-inept and reclusive. So, what's causing her to act like this?

She walks down her street, clutching the books against her chest. Her mind, as they say, is racing a million miles a minute.

A man is standing in front of Maya's house when she turns around the final corner. He stops her from entering, waving a rolled-up piece of parchment at her. He's buff and hairy, with sleek black hair and a fair face. "Got this off the Cari—sailed all the way up from Klymora, apparently." He hands the parchment over, his curious eyes trying to read through the thin material.

Maya doesn't smile, snatching the letter from the courier. "Be on your way." The man huffs but continues on his route—delivering more letters and parcels to the people of her street.

She unties the thin twine and then unrolls the parchment. She knows she should stop after the first line, but meager curiosity drives her forward.

Dear Ayne,

I am writing to you because I know I acted foolishly. I regret not being there to say goodbye.

But I miss you—and I am sad that I missed the opportunity to tell you, once again, that you're beautiful and wonderful.

Because you are, truly.

Even though I can't see you now—I can sense your beauty from oceans away. From across the Abhainn, from before the Cari...

I wish this letter could remain good-natured, but things in Klymora have taken a turn...

My mother found out about your plans. I don't know exactly how; I can only assume Faramund was sent to spy on your family once again.

She's furious. The wedding alliance is still her main plan, but I fear she'll forgo it and wage war with Gaia.

To calm her irrational mind, please hurry back. The sooner you're here, the sooner we're married, the safer both our people will be.

I believe she's hesitant for now because of the depletion of our troops. But my mother never hesitates for long.

I hope this finds you in best regards, I will be writing again soon.

-Prince Talin of Klymora

(Penned in the Prince's Suite, Caledonia)

Maya looks up from the letter and blows out a quick breath. She swallows, tightening her fist around the parchment, listening to the satisfying crinkle of the distant prince's writing.

When King Ren wrote to her, he told her to train Ayne, to not send her back until she's ready.

She shoves the letter into her pocket. If Maya is considered anything, it's a woman of her word.

CHAPTER SEVEN

The Book

Maya walks through the open front door, one hand resting in her pocket and the other clutching her books.

Mason looks up from the couch, where he's studying a book of Zhongguonese maps. When he sees it's Maya, he stands sending the book clattering to the floor. He blushes, "afternoon, Maya."

Maya nods in response, brushing through the living quarters and toward her room. Lio catches sight of her, having just come out of the lavatory. She grins broadly. "Hi, Maya. Ayne and I will be playing with the new gerbil in our sleeping quarters if you need us. We think it's a girl." She shrugs.

"How wonderful," Maya says, not able to keep the strain out of her voice. Lio doesn't seem to notice; if she does, it doesn't faze her.

When Maya's alone behind her door, she lifts the thin sheet off Nikolai's painting and sits on her bed, his oceanic eyes stare back at her. The ingredients she bought from Marinette the day before sit in rows on her dresser. She flicks her hand, lighting the lone candle and illuminating the room.

Maya stares back at Nikolai's portrait before dropping the books on the bed beside her. She flips to the first page of *Secrets of Magic*, eagerly awaiting the answer to why her magic would react like that and why *Ayne* reacted like that.

Maya begins to read:

> *A witch is a woman, just like a sorcerer is a man, who draws from the atmosphere around them to create something others believe is impossible. In this book, you'll go deeper into the world of magic, learning things most witches and sorcerers don't know themselves.*

Maya's face is creased in concentration. She knows what she's looking for, she just needs to find it. She flips to the chapter that holds the most promise:

> *Unusual Moments of Magic.*
>
> Chapter 12: *Unusual Moments of Magic*
>
> *When a witch or sorcerer experiences a moment where their magic is completely uncontrollable, they can then know that they're in the presence of a spirit or demon. Spirits are deceased beings straining their connection to the living to help a single person, or on rare occasions many. A demon is a ghost brought back to do evil. Another difference between a demon and a spirit is that you (unless it is you they are attached to) cannot see a spirit. You can see a demon. The only way you can determine that someone is a demon and not a member of the living is by the reaction of your magic. If being around them constantly triggers your magic (usually resulting in fire/explosive outbursts) then they are a demon. There are half-demons as well, that's when a demon is trying to drag a living soul into the world of the dead and take their body as their own.*

Maya meets Nikolai's eyes from across the room. Even though he isn't here with her—even though he's just a painting—she can almost hear both their heartbeats quicken with this new revelation.

When she first saw Ayne, nothing happened—

nothing unusual. Only after she transformed the raccoon into a gerbil did she start acting weird. Did that have anything to do with it? It seemed as if she were talking to someone...someone Maya couldn't see.

Maya stares at her floor. Is Ayne connected to a spirit?

"Good morning," Maya says, sitting down at the table outside. Lio is playing with Bao in the yard, tossing a lemon back and forth, giggling. Maya doesn't see how it can be *that* funny. Mason is already sitting at the table, drinking eagerly from a glass of lemonade. Ayne is too.

Ayne swallows quickly and dips her head in greeting. "Good morning, Maya. Did you sleep well?"

Maya's too busy studying her apprentice—watching the air around her as if she can catch sight of the ghost. So far—no luck.

"Ahem?"

"Yes?"

"Did you sleep well?" she repeats, taking another long sip to fill the silence between her question and Maya's answer.

Maya rests her elbows on the table and leans forward. "No, I didn't. I...had things on my mind."

"Like what?" Mason asks, his face etched with something close to concern.

Maya smiles at that. A man she just met is concerned for her? How outrageously delightful. And outrageously ridiculous.

"It doesn't matter. We have other things to worry about today." Her eyes drift back to Ayne. Who is the spirit that is attached to her?

"Another lesson?" Ayne pipes up, twisting her hair away from her shoulders to reveal Caz and a small brown lump, enveloped in peaceful sleep. "I think I'll give her to my sister. In fact, she looks just like the earrings I got for her! Such a coincidence, right?"

Maya shakes her head slowly. "It probably isn't a coincidence. When you were asked to transform the raccoon, your mind probably went back to the earrings. That small gerbil is the earrings in living form. Interesting, isn't it?"

Ayne looks ecstatic. "That is so…"

"Interesting?" Mason supplies.

"Very, very interesting," she agrees, nodding her head rapidly.

Maya nods as well, leaning back in her chair, far enough to blind herself with golden morning sunlight. She can hear a knock on her door from the backyard. Her eyes instantly widen.

"Don't worry, I'll see who that is," Mason says, standing and pushing in his chair. He straightens the collar of his white button-up and smooths down the wrinkles in his sleeves before reaching for the door to head back inside.

Maya springs from her seat. "No, no! I'll see who it is." She tries to compose her expression—desperation is a cause for curiosity. She doesn't want Ayne to be curious about what she can't let her see: the letters from Prince Talin.

"Are you sure?" Mason asks, his hand still resting on the door, an eyebrow irked.

"Yes, I'm quite sure. You're my guest. Allow me," she explains, gently pushing Mason away from the door so she can open it. She looks back over her shoulder at him. "Go sit back down, enjoy your lemonade. I'll tell you if it's anything important." The lie is so smooth on her tongue, it makes her question her morals.

She meets the courier at her front door—the same man as the day prior.

"An official letter from Emperor Neo. Everybody is receiving it." He hands over a rolled parchment, held together by blood-red string and a wax seal depicting a native Rose finch. The chosen seal of Emperor Neo. Every emperor chooses a new seal when they take the throne.

"An official letter?" Maya asks, even though she already knows it is. It's just been a while since the emperor involved the entire country.

The man nods in confirmation.

She doesn't wait for him to leave. She tears it open, eager to find out what's so important—eager to find out what her emperor has done.

Dear Zhongguonese citizens,

I, Emperor Neo Zhang, am officially announcing the closure of all trade routes connected to Zhongguo. All vessels currently departing or arriving will be sent back to their country with the same note. All merchandise ordered from other countries that have yet to arrive will be sent back.

There will be further announcements pertaining to this decision.

Xiè xiè,

-Emperor Neo Zhang

(Penned in the Emperor's palace, Beijing)

Maya's face crinkles. Her mind teases between theories of why he would do this. But she's too confused and concerned to land on any particular one.

CHAPTER EIGHT

The Reveal

"They closed the trade routes?" Ayne asks in disbelief, snatching the letter from Maya's hands to read it herself.

"Yes," Maya explains, sitting down at the backyard table again. This time she brought a pitcher of ice-cold lemonade with her. She refills their glasses and takes a sip from her own.

"But why? It took Zhongguo and Gaia forever to establish them. Why would he break it off now?" Ayne nibbles on her bottom lip, staring at the ice cubes bobbing in her glass. "It doesn't make sense."

Mason rests his hands around his glass, enjoying the cool touch on the warm afternoon. "I've read history books about this. Usually trade routes are closed when they're on unfriendly terms with certain countries. Did it specify which countries?"

Maya shakes her head, taking a long drink. "No. It just said all trade routes are closed."

Ayne nods in agreement.

"Then are you guys unfriendly with *all* countries?"

Maya slumps back in her seat, pressing a hand to her forehead. "No. At least, the public wasn't made aware if we were."

"What about in Gaia or Klymora? Any rumors arising about hostility in Zhongguo?"

Ayne looks grave. "No. I've never heard any…" Her face pales and her hand that's cupping her glass starts to shake. The ice chips clink together.

Maya's hands' envelope in misty pink magic and she stands up abruptly from her chair, sending it crashing to the ground. She backs away from Ayne, whose own magic is rising from her fingers like smoke on a hot summer day.

The spirit and the closed trade routes, are they

connected?

Maya's eyes flash between Ayne and her hands. Maya's magic fades away and she gasps, the warmth from her magic was so intense. More intense than it's ever been before. "You're as white as a sheet, Ayne. Tell me why," Maya insists, still standing feet away from her apprentice.

Ayne pulls her eyes away from her glass of lemonade, reluctantly meeting Maya's gaze. "What? No, I'm fine. I assure you." Her voice wavers and she quickly looks away.

Maya walks closer to the table, resting her palms flat on the surface and leaning toward her apprentice. "Your assurance isn't believable, Ayne. Tell me, as your mentor. I insist."

"No, I can't—"

Maya slams her hand down, the lemonade in the pitcher splashes against the brim. A chorus of clinking ice chips follow. "I said *tell me*. I cannot have an apprentice whom I distrust. Ignore whatever is telling you to lie," she leans even closer, "be it your conscious or another person…" Her stare bores holes into Ayne.

Ayne sits up straighter, her eyes wide. "Person?" She looks down then back up and sighs. "Fine. Can you please keep this between us?" Her eyes dart between Mason and Maya.

Maya forces the temptation of a smile away. She's finally going to hear the truth. She sets her chair back up and sits down, clasping her hands across her lap. "Go on."

CHAPTER NINE

The Truth

Ayne splays her hands on the table in front of her, checking to make sure Lio is still in the yard playing with Bao, before saying, "I haven't even told my family this—not the whole story anyway. But..." Ayne tells them about Estanova Macellen, and how she's the reincarnation of the deceased Klymora princess. Ayne tells them about Estanova's curse, how the first child from every Edelweiss and Macellen generation are destined to be drawn to each other, and if they marry, then their kingdoms are foreseen to combine. She tells them, then, about her flashbacks, how her vision seemed to switch between her present and Estanova's past. And how no one else can see her.

"When I was leaving Gaia, starting my voyage here, she appeared again. She said 'Soon, when the three warring countries unite—then there will be a sacrifice.'" Ayne sighs. "I can only assume she means Zhongguo. What other country could she possibly be referring to?"

"And that's why the trade routes are closing..." Mason says, shaking his head in astonishment. "That makes sense. He's preparing for war." He looks between Maya and Ayne. "I can't believe it..."

"But Gaia and Klymora aren't at war anymore," Ayne mumbles, staring at the table. She straightens up, positioning her hands on her lap. Caz thumps his feet on her shoulder and squeaks something angrily. But she keeps her face stoic. "Well, Talin and I aren't married yet, so technically the war isn't officially over." Her eyes flicker between the faces of Mason and Maya. "Soon, the war *will* be over. Completely over. I will marry Prince Talin before his fifteenth birthday, and I will save my people. Zhongguo won't have a chance to join the war." The hard set of her face makes

77

Maya and Mason exchange a look.

"But what if they start their own war? What could they possibly want from Klymora and Gaia?" Mason asks.

Mystified, the three take a long drink from their glasses, staring at the half-full pitcher of lemonade. The sunlight that bounces off the ice chips in the pitcher reflects into their eyes, but they don't turn away.

CHAPTER TEN

The Mentor

Maya circles Ayne, her exposed toes grazing the warm grass. It's still summer, but not for much longer, so she still has an excuse to wear sandals. It's been a while since she's felt the grass beneath her feet. She remembers a picnic she went on with Nikolai, a year after they met—down by the Cari, watching the waves lap against the docked ships. She remembers how her face hurt at the end of the night from smiling. It's been a while since she's smiled, truly smiled, that much.

Lio, Mason, Bao, Caz, and the small female gerbil stand off to the side, a safe distance away from the witches.

"Are you ready?" Maya asks, stopping in front of her apprentice.

Ayne bites her lip, clenching and unclenching her hands; a long crease etched into her forehead. But she nods. "Yes, I'm ready."

Maya bows her head. "Good." She clasps her hands in front of her, her short black hair pinned away from her face—including that pesky strand that insists on tickling her during the worst times. She's wearing a long blue dress with ribbons tightened around her waist. The gentle summer breeze catches the hem of her dress.

"What exactly are we doing today?" Ayne asks.

Maya holds her hand in the space between her and Ayne, allowing a gentle flame to dance across her palm. "I want to see how long you can just hold your magic. Don't do anything else."

Ayne frowns. "I can't control it—let alone hold it. I've told you that. That's why I'm here."

Maya copies her frown. "In order to get better at things, Ayne, you need to try them." She drops her hand back to her side, expelling the flame. "If you can hold your magic without releasing it, then you have control over it. Now, let's see."

Ayne takes a deep breath, readying herself to follow Maya's example. She lifts her hand up and presses her lips into a hard line. "Nothing's happening."

"Try again," Maya insists, taking a couple of steps back. "I know you can do it, Ayne. And, deep down, you know you can do it too."

Ayne takes another breath and nods. A small flame bursts to life above her palm, flickering for a few seconds before dispersing. Ayne grins, looking back up at her mentor. "I did it!" she announces.

Maya smiles. "Good job. Now, do it again. When your magic is threatening to overtake you, you'll feel an intense burning sensation. If you feel that, try to rein it back."

Ayne raises her hand again, forcing a purple flame to lick across her skin. It grows and grows until it's about the size of her head. Her smile dims and she shouts, "I'm feeling it! But I don't think I can call it back."

Before anyone can do anything, a ball of fire bursts

from her palm, ricocheting off the side of the house, leaving a black burn mark in its wake. Before it can barrel straight toward the lemon tree behind Ayne, Maya stretches her magic out and transforms the hurtling fire into ash. It falls from the air, sprinkling across the grass.

Ayne collapses to the ground, ignoring her dress as it crumples around her. Her eyes well with tears. "See! I can't control it. I thought I could, but look! I almost killed you all. I," she chokes back a sob, "I almost burnt your house down. I could have burned your precious tree down. What other things could I have harmed if you weren't here to fix my mistake? I can't do this."

Maya sits down next to her, rubbing a hand down Ayne's back. She smiles. "No, Ayne. Your magic isn't strong enough to burn down my house, let alone my tree. Not yet, at least. But by the time your magic *does* get strong enough, you'll be strong enough to control it."

Ayne covers her face with her hands, stifling her sobs. "I can't do this, Maya."

"Of course, you can do this. You wouldn't have this gift if you couldn't control it." Maya pushes

Ayne's hair behind her ear and lifts her chin up. "Look at me, Ayne."

Ayne blinks, wipes away her tears and looks up at Maya.

Maya sighs. "You *can* do this. Believe me."

"W—why are you so confident in me?" Ayne asks, wiping away more tears that threaten to drip down her cheeks.

"Because I was just like you. I couldn't control my magic, I didn't believe I would ever be able to, but then I met someone. He helped me train, he helped me perfect my magic." Maya sighs, dropping her hand to the grass, feeling the warm blades beneath her fingers and remembering him. "The more you train, Ayne, the stronger you'll be. Today is just the beginning, and every day after, you'll feel yourself grow. You'll feel the changes, the power, the control." Maya flickers her gaze up to Mason, a half-formed, dangerous idea coming to mind.

Ayne sniffles, running a hand under her nose. "Thank you, Maya. Thank you."

"Mason?" Maya asks, wiggling a finger for him to step forward.

Mason lifts an eyebrow, stepping hesitantly toward

her. "Yes?"

Maya stands up and dusts off her dress. "Stand over here, Mason."

"Okay..." He positions himself.

"Ayne, let's try that again," Maya suggests, a smirk appearing on her face.

Ayne starts to protest, but is silenced by a stern look from Maya. She gulps, raising her hand back into position. "Okay—I'll try again."

Mason's eyes widen and he shakes his head, filled with panic. Maya's diabolical plan becomes increasingly obvious.

"Wait! Are you sure this is safe?" Lio asks.

Maya chuckles. "No. I am not sure. But, if earlier was any indication, I *am* sure I'll be able to stop it if it gets out of hand."

Ayne steadies herself, focusing on her open hand, summoning a ball of magical fire. It grows quicker than last time, quicker than she expects, and quicker than she can control. It hurtles from her hand, zooming straight toward Mason.

The light emanating from the ball of fire cloaks his face in purple—coloring his fear. His wide eyes, his quivering lips, and his flushed complexion, are all highlighted. Ayne struggles trying to reign in her magic, but all it does is cause the ball of fire to zig-zag across the yard.

A scream rips from Ayne's throat as she tries to lower her arm, trying to break her connection to the wild flame. "Stop it, Maya! Stop it before it hurts him!"

Maya smiles, watching the burning blaze inch closer and closer to his face. If it touches him, he'll be thoroughly burned. "No," Maya exclaims. "You need to stop it. Draw on every ounce of magic within you. Make it stop. Make it come back to you. Do that, or he gets hurt." She scans the horrified faces of her guests, making her smile widen with each one. "Sometimes you need to learn and grow by facing your fears. I certainly did."

Sweat and tears mix on Ayne's face like paint on a canvas. She grits her teeth and closes her eyes—either concentrating on stopping it, or looking away before he can erupt in agony. She lifts her hands, choosing the former.

"You are not someone who allows others to be hurt," Maya whispers, urging the words to get through to Ayne. She doesn't want Mason to be scarred—but what will Ayne learn if Maya jumps in and saves him?

She needs to learn to do things on her own, she needs to learn to control her gift.

At the very last second, right before the ball of fire consumes Mason's face—Ayne opens her eyes and screams a flurry of inaudible words. The magic stops, and retreats.

Maya grins. Lio collapses in relief. Mason runs to hug Ayne. And Ayne stares at Maya, mouthing the words: *I did it*.

Maya nods. *Yes.* Yes, you did.

CHAPTER ELEVEN

The Lesson

Maya pulls back the curtains in the living quarters, the moon is barely visible among a blanket of storm-gray sky. Another signal—besides the dropping temperatures—that summer is nearing its end. Autumn is fast approaching. She's been informed by Ayne that the wedding between her and Talin is supposed to take place in early spring. It seems like a long time away, but time is a variable that runs out surprisingly fast. Summer will be upon them again in the apparent blink of an eye.

Maya lets the curtains drop, blocking her little home off from the rest of the world, just as she likes it. She moves to sit down on the floor in front of the fireplace, watching a small flame leap across a piece of kindling. Ayne looks up at her from her spot on the floor a few feet away. She cradles Caz in her hands before gently setting him back on her shoulder.

Maya pulls out the bottle of Essence she had stuffed in her dress pocket, placing it in the space between her and her apprentice.

Ayne studies the bottle of purple and blue smoke, twisting together in a foreign dance. "What is it?" her voice is delicate like she might scare the exotic substance.

"This is Essence," Maya explains, gesturing to the bottle. "It's pure magic, the only kind that can be captured. It's also very rare and in high demand. I was incredibly fortunate that Lady Marinette could get it for me. Buying it elsewhere would've cost a lot more than a secret."

Ayne's eyes flit between the bottle and Maya. "That's *magic*?" she exclaims, pointing a finger at the bottle.

"Yes, weren't you listening?"

Ayne scowls, crossing her arms. Caz thumps his feet on her shoulder. "Yes, *I was listening*. I just—I've never seen anything like that before. I've never seen magic so..."

"Beautiful? Pure?" Maya suggests.

Ayne shakes her head. "Peaceful. It's like looking at the Abhainn lap against the shoreline." She swallows her awe, and asks the question most people usually do when they discover Essence: "How is that possible?"

Maya smiles. "A long time ago an incredibly talented witch named Zaina Lee discovered how to bottle her own magic, since she had so much of it, and it was so pure. There wasn't a single evil thing about her, most would say. She's the only one throughout the history of witchcraft who's been successful at it. It requires immense control, and most witches don't have that kind of control."

"Zaina Lee?" Ayne asks. "Is she your grandmother?"

Maya chuckles, shaking her head. Her hair sways with the movement. "Great-grandmother actually. In fact, this town is named after her. That's why it draws all the gypsy folk and hidden witches and sorcerers in."

"What can it do? Why would your great-grandmother want to bottle it to begin with?" Ayne asks.

Maya turns her attention back to the fire. It's completely engulfed the kindling now, turning it to ash. "She wanted a way to help future witches control their powers, to benefit them and the people around them. Essence is used to control magic, Ayne. When you drink it, you'll receive the incredible control she had over her magic until it passes completely from your system."

Ayne's grinning from ear to ear. "I didn't know something like that existed. That sounds too good to be true."

Maya taps the cork of the bottle. "Yes, I know it does. But this here is only one dose. Save it until you truly need it."

Ayne nods eagerly, scooping the bottle up from the floor and sliding it into her pocket; she's wearing another dress on loan from Maya's younger days.

A knock sounds about the house and Maya jumps from her spot, opens the door, and disappears outside before Ayne can ask any questions.

Maya stares at the courier, ripping the letter from

his hand before he can even extend it fully.

Thankfully, however, he's caught on to the protocol: walk away and don't bother her with idle conversation.

The man mutters something about rude behavior under his breath as he trudges up the street.

Maya ignores him, quickly unraveling the letter and devouring each word that's sprawled in neat penmanship. It's not a letter from the emperor as she expected, instead, it's another letter from Talin.

Dear Ayne,

I hope you received my last letter. I'm writing this one shortly after. There are rumors arising in Klymora about Zhongguo. Apparently, Emperor Neo is talking with my mother and your father about closing the trade routes. Something amiss is going on. Please be on guard, I need you back safely. This may be my last letter to you—depending on if the rumors ring true.

-Prince Talin of Klymora

(Penned in the Prince's Suite, Caledonia)

Maya registers the sound of the door opening and closing behind her too late, too focused on reading the letter. Ayne peers over her shoulder, her hand grazes Maya's back, making Maya jump, crumpling the letter and stuffing it in her pocket simultaneously.

Maya scowls at her apprentice. "I thought you were a princess. Princesses have basic rules of etiquette, and I'm sure one of them pertains to reading someone else's letter." She can feel the hypocrisy in her words, like a boulder resting on top of her chest. Heavy, yet unmoving.

Ayne backs away, appearing thoroughly scolded. The little crease between her brow she gets when she's confused or ashamed appears, tenfold. "I apologize. But, was that from Talin?"

"What makes you say that?" Maya snaps.

Ayne winces, turning a cheek away from her mentor. "Never mind. I just thought I saw his name on the signature line, that's all."

Maya reaches out and takes Ayne's hand before she can head back inside. Remorse claws at her heart. Making her feel sick for lashing out at her, especially since Maya's the one doing something deceitful. "He's warning you and your friends about the trade routes ending with Zhongguo. Apparently, Emperor Neo, King Ren, and Queen Stella had discussed it."

Ayne blinks, the crease deepening between her eyes. "Did he mention why? Does he know if they're going to war?"

"That's all he said," Maya says. "Shall we go back inside now? It's getting awfully chilly out here."

Ayne starts to turn around until her gaze gets pinned to something behind Maya.

Maya follows her line of sight, all the way to the familiar figures crossing the street from the food market. Lio and Mason are laughing. They come to halt next to the two girls.

Mason looks at their expressions, clutching the bag of food tighter in his hands. "What's going on here?" A single eyebrow raises. "Did something else happen…? With the emperor?"

Ayne shakes her head, facing Mason and Lio. "Talin sent us a letter, warning us about the trade routes ending. But, so far, no one knows the real reason why."

"Exactly," Lio exclaims, shaking her head in exasperation. "Why is life so complicated? I mean, wouldn't it be nice if everyone just lived in peace?" She looks out at the street, where people on horses trot along, where a couple exchange sweet words, where no one seems scared at all. "Wouldn't it be so much better if nothing bad ever happens, to anyone?"

Maya watches the amorous couple as well. "It would be. But, sadly, that's not life. That's *The Above*. All the people who do good here will be rewarded up there," she explains, pointing to the darkening sky.

"Really?" Lio asks, looking up at the sky as well.

Maya only responds with a simple nod.

"What does Emperor Neo want?" Ayne says, but in a tone that sounds more like she's thinking out loud, not actually asking a question. "He must want something big. Big enough to challenge two countries at once." She turns her head slightly, listening to something—or, as Mason and Maya know—*someone*.

"Lio, can you unpack inside?" Maya asks, turning to the youngest. Whatever Estanova is telling Ayne now, she needs to hear it.

Lio huffs exaggeratedly, rolling her eyes. "Fine." She takes the food from Mason and heads inside.

"What did she tell you?" Mason asks before Maya can.

Ayne holds her palms out in front of her, as if to

calm a panic that isn't there... "Estanova told me what Emperor Neo is after... I don't know *how* she knows."

"Tell us exactly what she said," Maya demands.

Ayne begins, "She said 'it should be easier than this to discover. Gaia wants to keep the northern plateau. Klymora wants to take it. It's all about land...expanding their territory. Emperor Neo wants to take over Gaia and Klymora. He wants to expand Zhongguo.'"

CHAPTER TWELVE

The Announcement

The next day, before the moon fully disappeared, another knock echoes around Maya's house.

Maya darts upright in bed, her hair matted against her head and her eyes unfocused with sleep. She rubs a hand down her face and sighs. *This early?* She slides out of bed and kicks on a pair of slippers, shuffling to her door.

Maya attempts to open the door to her sleeping quarters quietly, but it's unsuccessful and a loud *creak* follows suit with the echo of the knock.

She sneaks into the living quarters, padding lightly

as to not wake Mason on the couch, but apparently, the knock already did.

Mason sits up, yawns, and locks eyes with her, tilting his head ever so slightly. "Do you want me to get it?" he mouths.

Maya shakes her head, offering him a small smile as a thank you. She actually would prefer him to open it, it's too early to be receiving anyone. But, what if it's another letter from Talin? If Mason found out that she's tucking away Ayne's letters, he'll tell her. He is her loyal courtier after all. Then, as a result, all the trust built between Maya and her apprentice would be broken.

She opens the door with a frown plastered on her face. She hates being seen in her night clothes. She's embarrassed enough that Mason saw her in her long, lacy, pink nightgown.

The courier passes her a scroll.

"This early?" she groans, glaring at him as she accepts it. She looks down at the parchment, and the emperor's royal seal catches her eye.

"By demand of the emperor," the man explains, giving her a *this-is-ridiculous* kind of smile.

Maya steps back inside without replying. She tears

at the seal, ripping it completely off, along with bits of parchment.

Mason is waiting for her, arm on the back of the couch, chin in hand, eyebrow lifted.

She sits down beside him and he scoots closer. His thigh brushes hers. It's warm, and not entirely unpleasant—which confuses her. It *should* be unpleasant! She should want to move, to break contact, to hide. But...she doesn't.

Mason reads the letter over her shoulder.

Dear Zhongguonese citizens,

Continuation of closing the trade routes: the Zhongguo militia is already sailing to the neighboring country, Gaia. From there on, they will breach both Klymora and Gaia borders and seize the land beneath the palaces. After the planned victory, a small number of Zhongguo citizens will be chosen and brought to each land—there they will re-colonize. The colonizers will be chosen at random.

Every citizen is ordered to submit an identification statement—those failing to comply will be brought in by force.

Xiè xiè,

-Emperor Neo Zhang

(Penned in the Emperor's palace, Beijing)

Ayne reads and rereads the letter, with every pass her face scrunches more. She shoves it across the table and shakes her head; her eyes contain rage and sorrow, fighting with each other for dominance.

"He can't do that!" she growls, slamming a hand on the table. "He can't just invade Gaia! My people won't stand for this."

"Yes, I'm afraid he can. He's the emperor, Ayne. That title holds that kind of power," Maya explains—even though she doesn't want to admit it herself. She closes her eyes, pressing the heel of each hand against them. "If there is one thing I know about my neighbors: it's that they don't like to be told what they can and can't do," Maya says.

"This is going to turn ugly, incredibly fast," Mason says, voicing the thought bouncing around Maya's head. "Is there anything we can do to stop it? He can't just rehome people like that, without giving them a choice in the matter. And he certainly can't invade Gaia and Klymora. They'll go to war and countless innocent people are going to die."

Maya shrugs solemnly. "The emperor will never listen to anyone below him—therefore he'll never listen to anyone. Everybody knows it, he's too caught up in his title. He's a tyrannical leader," she levels her eyes with the group, "he's going to destroy Zhongguo and force everybody to sit around and watch."

"I can sense an 'unless'," Ayne says hopefully.

Maya nods once. "Unless everybody bands together to show him what he's doing is wrong. I know my people won't—at least, not enough. But I have a plan. It may not work, but it's worth a try."

"What does it require?" Ayne asks, leaning closer.

Maya shifts in her seat, biting her lip. "You, me, and magic."

CHAPTER THIRTEEN

The Shadows

Maya is standing next to Ayne, facing the back of her house. Lio and Mason are standing safely behind them, along with Bao, Caz, and the unnamed female gerbil.

Maya thrusts her hand out in front of her, using her magic to steal the shadows created by her house. She grits her teeth and a drop of sweat slips down her forehead. She's trying to twist the shadow, to carve it into a creature of her choosing. With a determined grunt, she lets go of the shadow. A smile plays across her lips when a life-size bunny hops in a circle in front of her, made entirely by the shadow created by the brief lightning that flashes across the sky. It grows bigger with every hop; soon, however, there's a menacing jaw full of pointy fangs, large feet studded with claws, and a giant hole in the center of the creature's face, where an eye glares back at them.

"Is that what we're doing?" Ayne asks, taking a step away from the monster. "Is it going to hurt us?" She looks nervously back at Caz.

"Yes, this is what we're doing today. And no, it won't hurt us. I control it—it'll only do what the creator demands." Maya tugs her hair into a ponytail, a few stray, black tendrils frame her face, and red glitter sparkles on her eyelids. "We'll be melding the shadows. Now you try. All you have to do is imagine your magic as a glove around your hand. Reach toward the shadows, pull at them, play with them, form them. They'll be cool to the touch and they'll feel like they're constantly moving between your fingers."

Ayne swallows, and looks over at Maya, then nods. "Okay…" she says. She steadies herself on the earth, then juts her hands toward the wall of shadows before her. She bows her head, a bead of sweat drips from her brow from the strain.

Maya watches the shadows crawl off the building, slinking across the grass in unsteady bounds. As soon as they reach Ayne, her concentration breaks.

"They touched you, didn't they?" Maya asks.

Ayne's large eyes find Maya's and she shrugs slightly. "I don't know… It was cold and felt like water running over my skin." Her fingers rub her knee; she shakes as if the tendrils are still touching her.

Maya pushes an exasperated breath out. "It's a start, but you're going to have to get better."

Over the next week, Ayne and Maya practice in her backyard for hours—only stopping when the light leaves them. Ayne gets much better at controlling her magic: admiring it dancing across her fingers for longer periods of time. They don't work on transformation again—it being such a small spell, and other things claiming higher priority. Her animated shadows grow in strength and height. With every second the lumbering creatures remain, Maya's confidence in her apprentice grows.

At last, the day arrives when Ayne is proficient enough to attempt Maya's plan.

Ayne runs a brisk hand over the ice-cold balcony of an old building in Beijing. Her breath clouds in front of her. She wraps a crimson scarf around her neck and turns to a set of dark brown eyes staring back at her.

The last time they spoke was on the carriage ride from Zaina—when Maya explained her entire plan.

"Are you ready?" Ayne asks, lifting an inquisitive brow.

"I should be the one to ask you that," Maya responds, looking over the city—the emperor's palace looms in the distance, golden with glory.

"That may be so. But you still didn't answer my question," Ayne says then wraps the scarf around the lower half of her face, only exposing the tip of her nose, which turns a bright pink.

Maya squints into the gray sky. She sticks her hand out, catching the first drops of chilly rain. They slide across her palm before plummeting to the street below. "There's a storm coming, Ayne."

Ayne chuckles, leaning over the railing to study the sky. "In more ways than one—some would say."

Maya clicks her tongue—a ghost of a smile parting her lips at the thought of the storm they're going to bring to Emperor Neo. "Some would say, indeed."

The sky starts crying. Waterfalls of harsh rain splash against the ground. A rumble of thunder follows a stark white streak of lightning that cuts through the sky, like a knife through soft butter.

Ayne's face is set with determination. "I'm ready to do this." She glances over at her mentor. "Just tell me when."

Maya smirks, pointing to the thin outline of the gates surrounding the palace. They open; the guards switch patrols. "Now."

Ayne grabs the bottle of Essence that Maya gifted her a few days ago from her dress pocket. With a confirmative nod from Maya, she uncorks it and raises it to her lips. The magic disappears down her throat and her eyes widen. Magic, fresh, unknown, and powerful, courses through her veins, ready to be of use.

Ayne licks her lips, takes a steadying breath, then pushes her hands out in front of her, stealing the shadows created by the lightning and lanterns from all the buildings surrounding them. She shoves them across the city—straight toward the palace.

Maya can barely see as the streak of gray slips between the closing gates. *They won't know what hit them.*

"Remember what I told you, Ayne," Maya says, cinching her black cloak tight around her shoulders.

She pulls the hood up over her head.

"I do, Maya. I'll make a crowd gather in the palace courtyard to keep most of the guards distracted while you talk with the emperor," Ayne recites. "But, do you really think he'll listen to you?"

"He'll hear me, Ayne," Maya says, gripping the rail and staring across the stormy expanse, at the tall buildings, the rundown shops, and the palace. "He'll hear all of us. Do you want to know why?"

Ayne nods. "Why?"

"Because he doesn't want an uprising."

Maya leaves Ayne on the balcony. She pushes past the front doors of the building and starts across the wet road. Her footsteps are silent on the ground, but anyone who notices her can see the blatant intent; it's written in her posture, in the set of her face, in her cloaked outfit.

She strides through the city, ducking between houses, and through alleys until she reaches the palace.

She squats in the shadows—an unknowing weapon around her.

Ayne already has a mass of shadows inside the palace gates under her control. But this part—getting up close—is too dangerous. What if she gets caught?

Ayne's too young to take the fall—to take the punishment. Maya's mind runs rampant with worries.

Maya cranes her neck as shouts sound from inside the palace grounds, her insistent eyes searching for the emperor's private chambers, where he's resting now. They land on an elaborate window in the center of the palace, and the lanterns inside flicker with life. A balcony with golden statues on all corners is beside the window. And leading to the balcony is a door.

She raises her hands, collecting the shadows around her—leaving a strangely bright, unrealistic alleyway behind. If someone looked at it now, they would think it's a painting—perfectly without depth—without shadows.

Ayne's already successfully formed her crowd inside the palace courtyard, she can tell by the shouting, by the confusion on the guards' faces as they turn from their stations on the wall, watching the scene unfold beneath them.

Maya grunts as the shadows fly from her hands, stopping shortly before the gates. Using a skill she perfected out of sheer boredom and loneliness, she leeches the colors from the surrounding area and melds them with the darkness. She molds the shadows as if they're tangible clay, then paints them in her mind. First a single person—pale skin, dull brown eyes, a downturned mouth. Then a group of people. Women, men, children. She continues playing with her masterpiece—dotting the consistently growing crowd with dogs and a few stray cats. And, for the finishing touch, she clasps her hand around her throat. She hears a voice in her head: deep and masculine. Rough, textured. Not *her* voice—but theirs.

The guards standing on the wall start to notice, prying their eyes away from Ayne's small crowd—about five or six people lurking in the shadows of the courtyard, just to make the emperor and his guards question their safety, question *why* and *how* their palace got breached—it's never been breached before. Maya instructed Ayne, if she feels the guards are getting too close to her shadows, to release them and join the outside crowd for the big finale.

The guards on top of the wall lift their bows and spears threateningly. But Maya ignores them, until the guards standing in front of the gate turn towards her, golden helmets concealing the majority of their faces.

"What's all this?" one guard calls to the crowd, tightening his fingers around his spear. "Go on. Get!"

Maya moves her fingers, turning each of the shadows' heads in sync to stare at the man. Even the dogs. It's flawed and unsettling, but she can't do anything else, at least, not without Essence. But she gave her only bottle to Ayne.

The guard backs up a step and drops his spear. "What—?" His mouth, the only thing she can see, tilts down in a frown.

Maya, with one hand still around her throat, begins to speak. All their mouths move at once—a collective of figures with the same voice and the same words. "You can't hurt us."

The man shakes his head in disbelief. A group of his comrades gather behind him, weapons clutched in tight fists. The gate creaks shut as they file out.

Ayne must've depleted her crowd—meaning they got too close too soon. The emperor isn't out yet.

"Back away. Go home!" another guard shouts, pointing the sharp tip of his spear to the houses lining the street.

"Not until the emperor listens to us."

The same guard steps forward, holding his spear as if to run them through. "The emperor will not see you. Leave now or we will have to use force." His voice is loud and carries through the storm that's raging above them. Thunder rumbles across the sky, and a bolt of lightning shakes the earth.

Maya makes the crowd shake their heads in response. "We can't do that. We are here to talk to the emperor."

"You're not going to get your way. So, I suggest you give up and go home. I will not repeat myself," the guard growls.

When the group doesn't answer, he charges. The rest of the guards behind him do the same. Loud battle cries compete with the thunder.

Maya was expecting this: her people would never give in so easily. "So be it." She moves her fingers along the slight breeze; the guard reaches the crowd and is met with an equal opponent.

The guard rams his spear into a man's heart—a killing blow, if he was real. The shadow disappears, making the guard stumble forward. He looks up, his face drained of all color. "What the! What are we dealing with?" he mutters, dodging a right hook from a woman beside him.

He rolls out of her reach, popping up behind her. Maya can't make her turn around in time and he lands a solid punch to her face. She disappears as well.

With the guard stunned, Maya seizes her opportunity. She uses a small boy with black fringed bangs, tan skin, and baggy clothing. She sends his left foot into the guard's groins. The guard doubles over in pain.

"Should we try again?" the shadows ask.

The remaining guards who are sprinkled throughout the crowd share a look. The man closest to the one who went down nods. His voice trembles. "Yes—I think we should." Fright is the main emotion written in his eyes. He looks to another guard. "Tell the emperor."

"Everything?"

He nods; his posture is rigid; his hands are clenched in white-knuckled fists. "Everything." A muscle in his jaw twitches.

CHAPTER FOURTEEN

The Emperor

The doors leading to the emperor's personal balcony open with a flourish, and the emperor walks out, gliding toward the railing, a guard on each side, spears pointed toward the stormy sky.

Emperor Neo is a rather handsome man—if you only considered his exterior. He rests a gold-ringed hand on the railing. He's wearing a crimson robe also decked with golden threads. His dark brown hair is long and pulled into a low ponytail. His face is slender and his eyes are dark with mystery. He's smiling, a smile that sends goosebumps racing down Maya's arms.

"Speak," he calls, narrowing in on the crowd with falcon-sharp eyes. The guards behind him bang the bottom of their spears on the floor.

Maya obeys. "We came here today, to tell you that there will be consequences for your actions. You cannot get away with dis-homing your people," the collective says, turning to stare up at the emperor.

Neo barks a laugh. Not at all shaken by how perfectly synchronized the shadows are. Does he think they've just rehearsed it? Or does he already know what's going on? "Dis-homing? Please, my subjects, I am giving you a wonderful and rare opportunity. See it as the gift it truly is."

"It would be a gift if we were given the option to accept it or not. Something forced will never be seen as a gift. Usually, it's a punishment."

Neo rolls his eyes, waving their concerns away. "Who let you get this close to my palace?" He scans the guards looking up at him from the palace walls. "Who let this group of rebels get this close to me?" The guard behind him on his right whispers something in his ear, and his face twitches with rage. "Who let them slip into my palace? No one slips into my palace unless I want them to! Understood?"

He's saying something else too, words sewn between the lines: *who is going to be punished?*

Anger burns in Maya's chest. "Listen to us!" the shadows scream, their faces contorting with anger.

Neo's expression slips, revealing how stunned he is at their outburst. No one has ever spoken to him so harshly before, that much is obvious. His hand slips off the balcony railing. He straightens his robe, dusting something imaginary away. "I—I'll ruminate on your words. But, for now, head home."

Maya is panting with the energy of keeping the shadows in place. She can hear an underlying note in the emperor's voice: *he will not ruminate on their words.*

She can't hold on; she can see the shadows near the back of the crowd flicker. She's weak…how long can she hold on without giving herself away? The only reason they can't see her now is because she's hidden by the crowd. If she is seen…the emperor's punishment for questioning him will be deadly.

Maya lets a small groan slip, causing the crowd to groan as well. The emperor raises an eyebrow, his hands now clamped around the golden railing. "Good, because if you don't, we'll make ourselves known again." The shadows glare at him before turning to walk back through the alley. She strains even harder, trying to give them the impression of real people—different walks: some limping, others stomping. She disappears with them, weaving in and out of the crowd, her heart hammering inside her chest, knowing she just threatened the emperor...

Maya glances quickly over her shoulder, wiggling her fingers to make a few of the shadows around her do the same. Neo is still watching them until they're a satisfactory distance away. He disappears back into his chambers, the guards following suit. As the doors to his private chambers slam closed—a clap of thunder rolls across the sky.

A few blocks away, she can't hold on any longer. The shadows blink away, returning to their prior positions. She collapses against the cold, wet wall of an alley. She blinks once...trying to hold onto thin strings of consciousness. But they slip from her grasp.

CHAPTER FIFTEEN

His Moment

Maya looks up, her eyelids still feel heavy, and all her muscles ache. A clear blue sky is above her. And then a girl, staring down at her, tears pricking her eyes. Her long black hair tickles Maya's cheeks, and a weak chuckle escapes Maya's throat.

"Maya! Maya, are you okay?" the girl says, waving a hand in front of Maya's face. "It's me, Ayne. Here, let me help you up." She reaches down, wrapping her hands around Maya's arms, tugging her upward. But it's no use—Maya doesn't have the strength to move.

She collapses back, and her eyes roll down to look at a puddle beside her. Her hand twitches, stretching toward the puddle. Her fingertips graze the surface and she sighs. *The water feels nice.*

And then she's out again, being pulled into a world of darkness and dreams.

Maya wakes up in her bed, back in her home. Her head feels as if a ton of snails are crawling throughout it—blurring it with their slime. Her throat is dry and her tongue is like sandpaper. Again, her muscles ache.

Maya struggles to lift her hands, rubbing at her temples, trying to rid herself of an intense migraine. Her eyes gradually lift to Nikolai's painting. The white sheet isn't on properly, not how she left it. A corner is askew.

She groans, pressing the heels of her hands against her eyes. Her hands are cold and it feels nice. A knock pulls her from her thoughts—someone was in her room. Someone was snooping through *her* things.

Someone *saw* Nikolai.

Mason opens the door when she doesn't respond. A mug is cupped in his hand, a thin trickle of steam funnels the scent into the air. Mint and vanilla.

He smiles at her and takes a seat on the side of her bed, handing her the mug. "This will help you clear your head." He doesn't say anything else as she takes a tentative sip.

The tea coats her tongue, slipping down her throat. Her head feels immediately less foggy. "Thanks," she mumbles. His eyes are startlingly beautiful—since when has she considered them beautiful? She ducks her head. "You can go now."

"I—I actually want to ask you something," Mason says, rubbing his palms on his pant legs. His hair isn't in a ponytail, it's curtaining his face in sun-bleached waves. "When you and Ayne were gone. I had a lot of time to think."

She hates herself for being eager to hear his thoughts. A thin eyebrow raises inquisitively—*obviously* out of her control. She takes another sip.

He moves from rubbing his pant legs to fiddling with his thumbs. Still not looking at her. "I figured, I'd just ask. And then when I saw you unconscious—" He shrugs, shaking his head. His waves bounce with the movement.

She traces his figure with her eyes. Strong shoulders. Clear muscle. Yet still lean. She shakes her head almost inconceivably. Why is she looking at him like that? Since when does she care what her guest looks like? Since when does she care what he has to say?

Mason continues, "I was wondering if—"

Bao storms into her room, jumps up onto her bed, and wraps his arms around her neck in a grip so tight she struggles to breathe. "Bao, come on. Loosen up," she chuckles, excited to see her companion again.

Ayne stands in the open doorway, Lio beside her. She huffs, wiping a bead of sweat off her forehead. "He's been dying to see you since you got back. I've tried to keep him away and let you rest—but," she gestures to him and sighs. Caz squeaks on her shoulder as if he's agreeing with Ayne.

"Yes," Maya says, stroking Bao's soft head, "I know how persistent he can be when he really wants something."

"I think it's super cute how much he loves you," Lio exclaims, making a pouty face. "Can you tell us the story of how you found him?" She grins, perking up.

Maya smiles, cradling Bao across her lap. She trails her fingertips gently down his stomach. "Maybe one day." She knows she won't be able to tell the whole story…she can't find the strength to talk about Nikolai just yet.

"Come Lio," Ayne coos, taking the younger girl's hand. "She needs to rest." She cocks her head. "Mason, are you coming?"

Mason slumps forward, resting his face in his hands. He pushes out a slow breath and nods. "Yes." He stands and follows Ayne. His eyes meet Maya's as he closes the door; she can read his disappointment.

She leans back against the headboard of her bed, taking another sip of her tea. Her attention returns to the painting.

Is it disloyal of her to be disappointed too? Maya wonders.

CHAPTER SIXTEEN

His Retaliation

Maya sits crossed-legged on the couch, Mason beside her—a sort of tension lingers in the air between them. A tension she can't name.

Ayne and Lio share a look.

Ayne speaks up, "I'll let you tell them what happened since I was back at the building holding the shadows inside the palace gates."

"I love how casually you said 'holding the shadows'," Lio declares, mystified. "I'll never get used to all this magic."

Ayne smiles. "I don't think I will either. Not fully."

Maya clears her throat, gaining their attention. "The plan was to make the emperor change his mind or at least realize and care about how his citizens are taking this. How wrong it is."

"And did you?" Lio asks.

Maya shakes her head—not wanting to say the word. Not wanting to look into their faces as their hope deflates. "We can't focus on the negative. If we didn't do this, Ayne wouldn't have pushed herself in learning to control her magic. She was given a reason—a goal to meet. One within view." Maya wrings her hands through her hair, knotting it on top of her head in a sloppy bun. A strand of hair tickles her cheek—the same, persistent strand. "I'm proud of you, Ayne. You've accomplished quite a lot since coming here."

Ayne beams. "I wouldn't say it was all me, the Essence helped a lot. But, thank you very much, Maya. You're a great mentor."

"Essence may have helped, but you were still the one in control," Maya says.

"Really, do you—" Ayne starts.

Mason interrupts her, his voice bittersweet. A scowl creasing his lips. "Enough of the compliments—

can I hear the rest of the story? I want to know *everything*." He peers over at Maya. "I want to know why you came back unconscious." His expression—concerned eyes, pink complexion, knitted eyebrows—makes her turn into a puddle. Again, she questions why he has this effect on her.

Ayne glares at Mason. "Did you interrupt me?" She crosses her arms over her chest and lifts her chin. Anger ripples around her like waves in the water.

Mason appears to be a statue. Pale as can be. "I do apologize, Princess Ayne. It was out of line, especially considering I'm your courtier. I didn't mean it."

She huffs. "*Ayne*. You're my friend, just call me Ayne." She frowns. "But never interrupt me."

He half bows from his sitting position, still ghost-white. "I won't, Ayne."

Maya tries to diffuse the situation. She swivels to face Mason—ignoring the worms wiggling in her stomach. She begs her own complexion to behave. "I overexerted myself. Ayne held a collective of shadows inside the palace gates, as a distraction, but I went closer. I created a mass of citizens using my many hours of practice with shadow magic to make them look realistic. It was supposed to resemble a protest. I demanded to speak with Emperor Neo. His guards fought me. I fought back. And finally, he came out..." She frowns, twisting a lock of her hair between her fingers. "I would've argued more, but I couldn't hold on. If he saw all those people disappear, and me hiding behind them..." She tugs on the strand of hair. "I couldn't risk it...so I had to leave."

Mason lifts a hand...then drops it. A tentative smile playing on his rose lips. "You made the right call, Maya. What would've happened if he knew it was you?"

She lets go of her hair, intertwining her fingers together and leaning forward. She rests her chin on her knuckles. "I would be punished." Images of a guillotine flash through her mind—blood, fear, and chaos. He hasn't sentenced someone in a very long time. He's probably antsy.

Mason gulps, leaning back; his face turning even whiter.

Lio shifts in her spot, turning to look between the three. First at Maya, then at Mason, then at Ayne.

Ayne's staring straight ahead...the way Maya does when she's remembering something—or *imagining* something.

Before Maya can ask, there's a knock at the door. It's loud and assertive... Not the knock of the courier, that's for sure.

The dread building in Maya's stomach as she takes the final steps to open the door almost makes her double over. Why is she nervous? She's home safe—no one saw her.

Maya cracks open the door, peeking out at the men; two clad in red and gold. One has a stubbled outline of a beard. The other is clean-shaven. They both don't look happy, as if they went out of their way to knock on her particular door.

"May I help you, gentlemen?" Maya asks, leaning against the doorframe. She keeps it shut enough that they can't see inside. Her nerves sing.

"You're the witch, Maya Lee, correct?" the one with the beard asks. His voice is low and gruff.

Maya can't hide her surprise...she assumed this was about her identification statement—the one she never even bothered to turn in, nor write.

"Yes...?"

He clasps his hands in front of him, broadcasting a silver dagger sheathed against his arm plate. "We're going to have to insist that you come with us."

"I'm sorry...may I ask why?" Cold sweat slicks her skin now. Everything feels heavy. Her mind, weighing a thousand pounds, threatening to topple her over. Her tongue, glued to her mouth, and her nerves, yet again, singing a song that she wishes they wouldn't—a song of death and destruction, a song mirroring the sound of the guillotine. She feels like fainting; she gives in, allowing the doorframe to be the only thing holding her up. Something warm cups her arm and she notices him. Mason, attempting to hide her, to save her. He's warm against her and she finds herself not wanting him to let go.

"Who are you?" the clean-shaven guard asks. He moves, allowing them to become aware of the dagger strapped to his arm as well. It glints in the sun shining through a haze of gray clouds.

Mason straightens, towering half a foot over the guards. The muscle that bulges in his chiseled neck dares them to ask again.

The shaven guard takes a step closer; his steel eyes penetrate Mason's resolve. "When the emperor's guard asks a question. You answer." His breath is pungent.

Maya can feel Mason swallow and can hear the

sound of his confidence retreating.

"Mason...Bretman," he mumbles, but his hand wrapped around Maya's waist doesn't loosen, doesn't retreat—in fact, he holds onto her tighter, refusing to let her slip away.

His grip is comforting... A comfort she hasn't felt in years.

"Well, Mason Bretman, consider yourself warned; if you attempt to prevent the emperor from getting what he wants, then you'll be brought before him, as rebels are." Then his attention switches back to Maya, and she steals her eyes away from Mason, hardly even aware that she was studying him to begin with.

Maya takes a deep breath, steadies herself, and pulls out of Mason's grip. The absence of his warmth, of his hand, begs her to return. But, instead, she lifts her chin and glares at the guard. "What do you want with me?"

The clean-shaven guard looks down at her. She decides to focus on the streak of black hair plastered across his sweaty forehead and not meet his eyes. Not giving him a chance to discover the fear harbored within her. "You'll find out, Miss Lee. Please, come with us now."

A carriage stops in the street behind the guards, as if drawn to his very words. A pair of brown horses stomp and snort. The carriage is crimson, detailed with gold like everything that comes from the palace.

The door facing her opens silently, ominously, and Maya gulps.

She can barely make out his face through the tinted windows. Narrow and long. Arrogant. Thin lips, strong jaw.

The bearded guard turns to Maya, gesturing for her to walk forward. "The emperor is waiting, Miss Lee, and no one keeps the emperor waiting."

The sounds of Mason protesting behind her fade. She can't listen—she *won't*. With every step she takes toward her ruler, she can feel her fate begin to seal.

CHAPTER SEVENTEEN

His Punishment

Maya is strapped to a chair with leather cuffs binding both her wrists and ankles. Her arms are stretched around the back of the chair, pulling at her muscles. The sun blares through the window beside her, painting the room in a coat of flavescent.

A tree stands outside. It's green, slowly turning orange as the seasons shift. A leaf falls from the closest branch. She watches it sway on the subtle breeze. For once, she wishes she can be as free as that leaf, drifting away from everything and everyone. What would it be like to just be Maya Lee? A girl from Zaina, and nothing more.

Her eyes trail across the plush beige rug beneath her feet, across the golden walls, and land on two brown spheres with crow's feet.

Up close, his face is creased with wrinkles. Has anyone ever been this close to the emperor before? Any normal subject? But—then again, she isn't a normal citizen. She isn't a free leaf.

"Maya Lee," Neo whispers; her name on his tongue is like venom, straight from the fangs of a snake. She shivers as it drifts in the air between them, daring her to say something.

She barely remembers to address him respectively. If she's already in trouble, it might be best not to add to it. "Emperor Neo?"

Neo's lips twist into a smile…a kind smile. Yet his eyes hold the darkness she was expecting to find. His known malice. "Maya Lee, the only known witch in Zhongguo. It's been a while, hasn't it?"

Maya cocks her head. Her wrists strain against the restraints as if it's become a reflex already. "Has it? I don't remember having a conference with you before."

He taps his index finger against his cheek; he's bent

forward on his matching chair, paying attention to every word and action that her body makes, with eyes of a hawk and sharp features to match.

He's so close…she can smell the cinnamon drifting from his body. An interesting cologne.

"Don't you think there's a reason for that, Maya Lee?" He rolls his eyes to the ceiling, a chuckle escaping his lips. The hair along her arm stands on end. "The only *known* witch in Zhongguo…"

"Why are you repeating the same thing?" Maya asks—then, like a slap across the face, she realizes… He's telling her exactly what he means, she just has to read between the lines: *there's another witch.* "Who?"

He glares at her, gesturing to the room around them. "We are in a palace, are we not? And usually in palaces, there is royalty and the proper way to address—"

"Pardon me, Emperor Neo," she says, wincing as she realizes she interrupted him.

He folds his hands on his lap and shrugs aimlessly. "It's fine, Miss Lee." His hostile glare says otherwise.

Maya frowns, dipping her head in a bow. "I won't forget again, Your Majesty."

"Wonderful." He tugs a hand through his hair and

smirks. "Let's talk about Ayne."

Maya snaps her head up. "Can you repeat yourself, please?"

He grins, receiving the exact reaction he was hoping for. "The other witch in Zhongguo: Ayne Edelweiss, Princess of Gaia." He lifts a chipmunk of a brow. "Do you know of her?"

Maya successfully composes herself. "I have. Princess Ayne Edelweiss. Who hasn't heard of the heiress of Gaia?"

He chews on her words. Then decides to twist them and spit them back out. "Have you heard of Princess Ayne Edelweiss, the witch? Gaia's secret stashed away in my country?"

Maya frowns. "No offense, Your Majesty, but is there a point to me being here for this discussion?"

Again, the answer he was hoping for. He tents his fingers, reclining in his chair and crossing a leg over the other. "Yes. There is. Do you know about a little...*protest* outside my palace the other day?"

Maya refuses to give anything away. She keeps her face deadpan.

"That little protest was arranged and performed by Ayne—makes sense, doesn't it? A spy sent from a country on the brink of war to harass the emperor into changing his mind?" He gives her a look, asking for her thoughts on the matter.

Maya sputters. "You think it was Ayne?"

He splays his hand in the air, displaying a picture formed by his words: "Really think about it. I have...*sources*...that have warned me that this infiltrator is residing with you."

"And who is your source, Emperor Neo?"

The door at the far side of the room opens, a woman saunters in, a once dashing smile plastered across her face. Her dreadlocks waterfall down her back. A red dress cinches at her waist, billowing across her knees and dusting the floor.

Maya can feel the ice growing inside her. It encases her heart, her head, her thoughts... Preventing rational behavior. Usually, Maya considers herself a rational person. An inventive poem of Zhongguonese curse words fly from her mouth, ricocheting off Lady Marinette's stoic shield.

She stops beside the emperor, a bold coyness tainting the air around them. "Neo," she purrs, batting her eyelashes, "did I do good?"

Maya growls, thrashing against the leather cuffs,

knowing that it's no use. She glances, her eyes wide with unaddressed fear, to the windows. There are no curtains to create shade. The sun filters into the room unrestricted. Her wrists may be bound—but her magic isn't, she just needs to find a shadow, even the smallest one.

Clearly, the only way she can get out of these bonds is by magic.

And once she's out—she won't be in control of her actions. That manipulative, lying—

"Maya?" Marinette calls, a hand on her hip.

"What do *you* want?" Maya sneers.

Marinette sighs, dropping her hand. "I'm sorry it had to happen this way." She shakes her head, her tail of dreadlocks swishing.

"It didn't *have* to happen," Maya argues, baring her teeth at the gypsy.

Marinette clucks. "Yes, it did. I read it in the cards. The cards never lie."

Maya rolls her eyes. "Cut the—"

The emperor tilts his head, stopping her from finishing her sentence by reminding her that she's in the presence of royalty. He waves Marinette away, asking her to give them a moment to talk. With a solemn wave to Maya, Marinette disappears.

Maya smothers her contempt; as the door opens, it casts a faded shadow against the wall. Hopefully, it's enough darkness to undo these bonds. She stretches her mind to it, imagining grabbing strands of soft, flowing shadows. She can feel the chill slithering across her knuckles.

"As I was saying. I'm going to punish Princess Ayne. A rebel such as that cannot be permitted to remain in Zhongguo with their freedom intact." He flourishes his hand, so casually it makes her stomach revolt.

Maya sharpens her focus on the inching shadows—shaping them into a dagger. She plunges it beneath the leather binding constricting her right wrist. She sets to work, sawing gently, slowly, and quietly… The binding snaps, but she muffles the sound of her working with her voice. "But Ayne is innocent."

"Is she? Someone needs to be punished for such an act. People saw, Maya Lee. My guards. The neighbors. Not to mention how stories spread." He leans closer. "Someone needs to be punished. Do you have a suggestion?"

The second strap snaps. Both her wrists are free.

"Yes, I do." She takes a deep breath. "It was me. Punish *me*." And then she tells him the story, excluding Ayne's involvement.

As soon as she's done, two guards rush into the room, armed with spears. The emperor stands, eyes narrowed, studying her. Probably wondering exactly how powerful she is.

"Take her to the dungeons. I don't want to see her for quite some time," Neo orders.

Panic seizes Maya as one of the guards bends over to cut the straps constricting her wrists. What will he do when he finds out she already cut them?

The emperor opens the door, casting shadows on the wall. Her pulse jumps as she stretches her magic toward the shadows, desperately grabbing at them before the door can swing shut. She reels them toward her, twisting and flattening them. She smooths them around her wrists, straining to give them the appearance of the leather straps, praying that the guard doesn't look too closely.

The guard pulls a dagger from a sheath at his waist. The other guard says something, pulling his attention away for a split second as the blade of his dagger cuts through the first shadow. With his attention still on the second guard, he slices through the second shadow. Maya leans forward, flexing her hands in front of her as if they had just now been released. If the guard checks, he'll just see the already broken straps and assume that's what he cut through.

She lets out a barely audible sigh as the guards cut the cuffs around her ankles, happy that they don't know exactly how powerful she is…yet.

CHAPTER EIGHTEEN

Her Imprisonment

She doesn't know how long she's been trapped down here. The walls are overtaken by damp moss. The floor is splattered with concerning liquids from the resident before. Dirty, broken hands stretch through the bars of her cell—reaching for her. A touch of clean skin, a sensation they probably haven't had in a very long time.

The only reason she's even staying here, allowing herself to be mistreated is because it was either her or Ayne.

Maya is a woman of her word—a woman trust can be bestowed upon. She won't let her apprentice take the blame for something she did.

A man delivers a tray of food. Nasty slop splashes against the rim of the bowl. The canteen of water is more tempting, even though her stomach gurgles with the need for something more.

She unscrews the cap of the canteen and peers inside. Half full, of course.

Her lips caress the container; dry and cracked. The water is sweet and rejuvenating. She tips the canteen back, desperate for every single drop.

Once it's bone-dry, she tosses it aside. The sudden moisture in her mouth teases her: *don't you want more?* it seems to say. The liquid that encompasses the mysterious food looks appetizing. She reaches for the bowl. It's grainy, thick, and sour as it rolls into her stomach. But it's wet like water.

She starts to heave, holding herself with her palms against the cool concrete floor. Her body shakes violently with every effort to rid itself of something that should never have been eaten—let alone considered as food.

The sound of boots stomping on the hallway

outside pulls her from her stupor. She looks up, meeting the same eyes that condemned her.

"Let's have another talk, shall we, Maya Lee?" he says. Her name echoes around the dungeon.

CHAPTER NINETEEN

His Offer

Maya is bound back into the same chair with leather straps tied around her wrists and ankles. But, this time, she doesn't search for a speck of lingering darkness, for a speck of shadows, knowing her search would be fruitless. Even if it was, somehow, successful—she doesn't have the energy to hold any magic.

"How long was I in that cell?" she asks, hearing her own voice for, seemingly, the first time. She tries to reach for her neck, to feel her words vibrate under her skin. To confirm it's her that's speaking. Her voice is scratchy and hoarse. Her wrist reaches the barrier of the cuff that's pinning her arm behind the chair and preventing her hand from completing its task. A groan tears through Maya.

Her hair is wild and greasy, clumped on her shoulders—a sure sign that it's been more than three days.

Neo smiles. "A week, Miss Lee. And you would still be in there, but Marinette and I began to think. How can we use you to our advantage?" He drums his fingers on the arms of his chair. "I have a proposition for you."

Maya's expression wavers, drifting from absolute repulsion to curiosity. The single thought in her mind is loud and clear like she's screaming it: *anything for water*.

"A week," she croaks. She clears her throat and tries again. "You held me in there for a week, and you expect me to agree to anything?"

He considers this. "Yes, I do actually. I know it'll be in your best interest."

The door opens and a woman shuffles in. She's balancing a golden tray with a ceramic pot of tea and two cups.

The steam that rises from the pot draws her in. Hibiscus and lavender. A liquid so close that can quench her.

The woman places the tray on the table, then pours them both a cup, lifting Maya's up to her lips so she can take a drink.

Maya drinks the tea immediately. The scalding temperature burns, but the feeling of liquid gliding past her lips, over her tongue, and down her throat is too tempting to resist. As soon as Maya's done, the woman whisks the empty cup and the pot of tea away.

Neo studies her over the rim of his cup, through the steam. After a small sip, he continues. "My proposition is that you work for me. Join forces with the empire. A witch with such incredible abilities as yours can be an extraordinary asset."

"Why would I even consider that?" she snarls.

"If you work for me, you get the same luxuries all my men do. Private quarters in the palace. Infinite meals of whatever you desire. Warm baths. Clean water. And freedom. I won't force you back into the cell as long as you abide by my rules."

Even though her home has clean water and she can

eat what she wants when she wants it, the deal still tempts her. The guaranteed freedom tempts her. The single thought of not returning to that cell tempts her. She's going to have to play this perfectly.

"If I agree to work for you, can I make a request?"

This intrigues him. He leans forward, cupping his chin in the palm of his hand and resting his elbow on his knee. He's holding his hot cup of tea with his other hand. "Go on."

She begs her courage to not abandon her. "If I work for you, I don't want to live in the palace. Let me go back to my home. I'll do whatever you want, just from my own house."

He shrugs lightly. "Fine. If that's what it takes, I can accept. If you don't live here, however, you won't be reaping the rest of the benefits."

Maya smothers both her surprise and relief. This is the only way she can get back home without incurring even more of the emperor's wrath. "That's fine."

He shoves his free hand toward her, grinning malevolently. "Excellent. Welcome, Maya Lee, to my side."

She doesn't smile. She doesn't nod. She just gestures to the straps restraining her. "Now get these off me."

CHAPTER TWENTY

Her Return

Maya glares over her shoulder at the retreating carriage—red and gold in the distance, fading as the heavy fog takes root in Zaina. It's nearly autumn, after all, and the temperature is decreasing little by little each day.

She lifts a hand to open her door, but it flings open before she's able to.

Ayne's face is etched with worry. She wraps her arms around Maya, burrowing her face against her chest. "Where were you?" she asks, pulling away from the hug to look into her mentor's eyes.

"It's a very long story, Ayne," Maya explains, stepping past her and into her house. The darkness that is usually so apparent is replaced by light, drifting through the open drapes, from lit candles on the mantle, and a warm fire. She breathes in the scent of ash and myrrh. "It's changed…"

Ayne nods excitedly. "It was too dark in here—we had to lighten it up a bit."

Before she can continue, Mason and Lio barrel from the guests' quarters. Lio squeezes her, tears pricking her eyes. Lio turns and runs a finger under her eyelashes, wiping away the few tears that managed to slip out. "I've been so worried! I haven't been able to sleep." She points to the purple bags under her eyes.

Maya caresses her cheek, it's warm beneath her touch. "I'm very sorry to have worried all of you—"

"I'll kill him," Mason growls, gritting his teeth. His face contorts with rage. "He had no right to take you away. What happened?"

Maya shushes him as quickly as she can. Her brown eyes are wide. "Never threaten the emperor. Even if you don't think *he's* listening—someone is." Her eyes flit around the living quarters as if an unwanted and untrusted person somehow escaped her attention.

He shakes his head, his blonde waves thrashing against his cheeks. "It's not acceptable."

"Acceptability has nothing to do with it," she insists, pressing a finger to his lips. Her eyes hold his, pleading with him to stop talking. To stop before he gets himself in serious trouble.

If she learned anything from her time in the palace, it's that you can't trust people, even if you think you know them.

"Please tell us what happened," Ayne says, taking a seat on the couch. She hugs her knees against her chest, locking her arms, waiting for Maya's story.

Maya sits down beside her. Mason and Lio follow suit—all squeezing onto the couch, embracing each other with the warm bump of a thigh or the brush of a shoulder; if Maya is positive about anything, however, it's that these three people she *can* trust.

Then Maya tells them what happened. *Everything*. From Lady Marinette's betrayal. Getting imprisoned in the emperor's dungeon. The feeling of helplessness. The proposal. And her new job.

At the end, everyone is silent. Absorbing her

words.

"I'm so sorry, Maya," Mason whispers into the quiet. He sounds defeated by *her* problems. She shakes her head. How intriguing, indeed. The quaky feeling in her stomach returns, feeling a lot like rabid animals being released inside her.

Ayne pats her arm, trying to conceal the concern that dances across her features. "We'll let you get some sleep. I can't begin to imagine what it was like, going through as much as you have." Her lips tremble and she looks to the floor. "And thank you for protecting me. You could've easily escaped, but you didn't to protect me."

Maya's lips turn up at the corners, a sadness lingering in her eyes. "Of course, I did, Ayne."

Ayne sniffles, running a hand under her nose.

Maya glances over at Mason as he wraps his arm around her shoulder. "Let me help you to bed—you must be exhausted." When Maya nods, he helps her stand up, letting her lean against him as they walk down the hallway, toward her sleeping quarters.

"Sleep well, Maya," Ayne calls after her.

"Yeah, sleep well!" Lio echoes, trying to refrain from sniffling.

Maya notices that her door is open a crack. Meaning that, yet again, someone was inside her quarters. She doesn't ask about it though. She finds herself not really caring if her friends went into her sleeping quarters while she was away.

Mason stops her in the doorway, his eyes locking with her own, his hand finding hers. "I'm sorry, truly, that you had to go through that..." he whispers. She can't pull her gaze away, let alone deny the fact that his voice makes her heart stutter. "But most of all, I'm sorry I didn't stop them. I wish I challenged them—I wish, with everything inside me, that I could've prevented this."

Maya looks down at the floor as heat rushes across her face. She already knows why she isn't pulling her fingers from his grasp. Why she isn't insisting on being left alone. Her eyes flit across his face now—his soft lips, his small button nose, and his startlingly beautiful eyes.

Eyes that remind her so much of Nikolai... A lighthouse in a storm. Bright and wondrous blue.

Maya slips her fingers from his grasp, pushing her door farther open. His warmth is suddenly absent and she finds herself wishing for it back. She swallows and turns to close the door, but his palm slams into it, pinning it open.

Maya steps back in surprise, her hand hovering above her chest. "What are you doing?"

His face is pink—she can almost feel the heat radiating off his skin—even though she's standing a little over a foot away.

"What I should've done sooner." He steps across the threshold, into her sleeping quarters. His strong hands find hers again, holding them in the small space between them. She can feel his breath against her cheeks. "Maya, will you allow me to court you?"

Her eyes dart to the covered painting of Nikolai. Her heart screams at her to say yes, but her brain hisses, insisting that it's betraying Nikolai...

But if Nikolai still loved her—wouldn't he be standing beside her right now? Wouldn't his hands be the ones clutching hers? Wouldn't it be him she is tempted to kiss?

But he's not. He's gone. He's been gone for far too long.

Maya pulls her eyes back to Mason's. Her words get stuck in her throat as they try to find volume. "Yes, you may court me."

His grin is like the scent of flowers, the sun turning the grass golden, the satisfaction of peeling bark off trees—everything nice and warm wrapped into something so small.

Her heart stammers again.

"Get some sleep, Maya." Mason smiles. "I'll see you when you wake up."

CHAPTER TWENTY-ONE

The Letter

The next day, after a handsome amount of rest, Maya opens her front door seconds after a knock sounds. Her stomach flips, and her nerves feel like they're on fire.

She can't help but expect the emperor's guards again. She can't help but be on edge.

"Another official announcement," the courier says, handing her a rolled parchment. The official stamp is bold on the pale paper.

"Thank you," she mumbles, her eyes already

enchanted by the words scrawled across the page. She knows he didn't personally write this—one of his hundreds of scribes did.

The man steps back. A mix of shock and curiosity is written in the creases of his face. "You're welcome," he says. His voice matches his appearance.

Maya retreats back into her home, closing the door behind her. Mason is already waiting, a coy smirk illuminating his expression. Yet she can still see the tinge of concern. "What does it say?" he asks.

Maya sits down on the couch, flicking a hand toward the fireplace. A hazy warmth cocoons her as the log inside the fireplace fuels a flickering pink flame. When she reaches the bottom of the letter, she can hardly believe she read it correctly. She scans it again.

Dear Zhongguonese citizens,

In light of yesterday's events—I have come to tell you that the palace has recruited the resident witch, Maya Lee, to help in the country's affairs. Her first assignment is enforcing strict identification statement submissions.

Be blessing Zhongguo with an early victory, my subjects.

Xie Xie,

-Emperor Neo Zhang

(Penned in the emperor's palace, Beijing)

Maya senses that this isn't just a letter to his subjects—this is a personal letter to *her*. Telling her what she has to do... Setting her people against her.

If they don't like being told what they can and can't do by the emperor, what would happen when their neighbor starts doing the same?

Maya pawns the letter off on Mason. She doesn't watch as he reads it. He reads it again to make sure he read it right.

He crumbles the letter in his fist. His brow is low

over his eyes. Anger seethes in every tense muscle. "What do you want me to do about it?" he asks. His jaw only relaxes as he meets her eyes.

She shakes her head slowly. "Nothing. There's nothing we can do. *I* made the deal. *I* have to pay the price." She drops her head into her hands, massaging her temples. "I should've seen this coming. Of course, he would do this."

Mason puts his hand on her shoulder, holding her close to him. He rests his chin on her head, closing his eyes.

Another knock resounds about the house.

Maya darts upright, springing from her seat to answer the door. Her fingers graze the cool metal knob, but she withdraws them. A loud chorus of shouting drifts through her windows. She peeks out the window, half hidden by the thick drapes.

A mob the size of the one she created in Beijing stands in front of her house. Angry fists pound the air. Zhongguonese curse words exchange lips. Eyes throw spears.

"I knew this would happen—just not so soon," she mutters, gesturing for Mason to take a look. He's behind her in a flash, craning to watch the crowd grow even bigger as more and more of her neighbors join.

His fingers dig into the skin of her arm and she flinches. Anger swims in his eyes...no, not anger. Rage. Pure and simple rage.

"I'll—"

"No," Maya says, stopping him before he can finish his sentence. "We can't hurt my neighbors."

"But they're harassing you," he declares, pointing at a woman sharpening a stick with a butcher's knife—carving it into an effective spear. "You can't just let them do this. Allow me to help. I'll get rid of them." He heads toward the door.

Maya grabs his elbow, forcing him to stop. She realizes the distance between them is slight. She pulls her eyes up to his. "Let me handle it. You go and wake Ayne and Lio. Tell them what's happening. Take them out back and stay there. I'll be with you shortly."

"You're being unreasonable," Mason chides, dragging a hand roughly through his hair. He sighs and looks back down at her. He's at least a foot taller. "They're obviously not here just to talk. If you get hurt out there, Maya, I won't be held accountable for what I'd do to them."

She almost smiles—almost. *I won't be held accountable for what I'd do...to protect you.* She can hear the unsaid words in the still air...echoing in her ears, bouncing in her mind.

She frowns instead, diverting her attention to her feet. "Mason, go." Her voice is hard—daring him to challenge her.

He swallows—it sounds weak and unsure. "Be safe, Maya." His words come out bittersweet.

The reality of her having to intentionally assure her own safety just by stepping into the street in front of her house is horrific, highlighting the misplaced cruelty Neo instills in his people.

Mason presses a kiss to her forehead. His lips are soft and tender against her skin. She blinks up at him, not wanting to look away even when his back is all she can see.

Turning back to the front door, she gulps, calming the nerves galloping throughout the entirety of her body.

She twists the cold knob open and steps into the sunlight. Her skin is pale, almost white in the clear morning light.

"Maya Lee," the woman with the makeshift spear

shouts, pointing her misshapen weapon at her. She bares her teeth, preparing to deliver a verbal blow. "You are a traitor to all of your neighbors. We trusted you. We thought you were a kind woman—sure, socially inept—but *kind*." She rummages around in the large front pocket of her apron. She pulls out the letter and crumples it in her hand, tossing it to the ground. "You destroyed that trust when you sided with the same man that's taking all our choices away from us." She shares a look with the rest of the crowd. Lifting her spear even higher, she screams, "We can't let her get away! Grab her!"

CHAPTER TWENTY-TWO

The Fire

Maya darts back inside the house. She slams the door closed and bolts it. Her magic buzzes with energy in her palms begging to be released after so much dormant time. Her energy is strong enough now to use her magic and it's a tempting thought, but she can't hurt her neighbors, she can't prove Emperor Neo right.

She closes the drapes quickly, then heads for the backyard, where she told Mason, Lio, and Ayne to go. Bao, Caz, and the unnamed gerbil are with them.

Mason's standing across from a sleepy Ayne and

Lio. He's talking with his hands, but his voice is low and soft.

Maya nears them. Her hand, following its own will, loops around Mason's arm. His skin is hot underneath the thin white linen shirt he's wearing.

Ayne's eyebrows shoot up. A smirk plays across her round face. "What's happening here?" Her eyebrows waggle.

Mason beams. "It's…fairly new," he explains.

Lio tilts her head. "I don't understand…" Then her face lights up. "Oh! Awe! That's so cute."

Maya waves them away, and the faint moment of happiness quickly fades. "Did you tell them?"

He nods sternly. His eyes falling to meet hers, then quickly flitting away. "Yeah. I told them. What do you think we should do? Surely, it's not safe…"

Maya agrees; the image of the woman sharpening her spear slips through her mind, leaving a trace of fear. "I don't know what we can do. We can't just leave— we have nowhere to go."

"Right…" He purses his lips. "Let's close the curtains, board the door, and stay in one room."

"That may be our only plan as of now." Maya turns back to study her apprentice's face. It's creased with panic, but her princess training still holds because confidence and hope linger underneath. "We're going to need help; the crowd outside doesn't look like it's going away any time soon."

Maya tears a part of her fence away—the section that's built directly against her neighbor's house, proving no other purpose than appearance. With nails in one hand and the board in the other, she makes her way through the house and to the front door where Mason's waiting to seal the outside world from them, and them from it.

Maya hands him the board, his fingers graze hers as he takes it, and she feels a jolt of warmth that courses through her body—making her heart pound quicker and her blood rush.

"Can you check on Lio and Ayne?" he asks, gesturing with his head toward the guests' quarters—the safest room in the house since it doesn't have a window.

"Of course," she says, starting down the short

hallway that branches off from the main one. She knocks on the doorframe, leaning into the room. Lio and Ayne moved the beds to the very back, so they immediately see anyone who enters. The dresser stands in the middle, like a barrier between them and anyone else.

Lio sits cross-legged on the her bed, smiling. She giggles when Ayne tells her a joke. Her voice is so quiet Maya can't make out the words.

"How's it going in here, girls?" Maya asks, walking around the dresser and kneeling in front of the beds. Ayne plops back on her bed.

"Fine. I do have a request though," she turns her thoughtful eyes on Maya, "can I pen a letter to my family? I know there aren't any ships going between countries right now, but, just in case..."

Maya shakes her head. "There won't be a 'just in case,' everything will be fine."

Ayne sighs, muttering, "Fine is just a word people use when they're hiding how they really feel..."

"What?" Maya cocks her head, scrunching her eyebrows together.

Ayne presses her lips closed and shakes her head. "It's nothing. It'll just make me feel better if I write one."

Maya pauses, then says, "I have paper and quills in my room. Be quick, I think it's safer if we aren't out of each other's view for too long."

Ayne nods and disappears down the hall.

Maya can hear her door squeak open and the floorboards in her sleeping quarters creaking. Ayne slides open the dresser drawer and begins to rifle around. They would be disturbing noises if she didn't know who was making them.

And then silence...

Ayne walks back into the room, frowning. She's holding a black quill and a small stack of papers. She lifts the first piece off the stack and shows it to them.

Maya's heart plummets. She raises her hand to her mouth without thinking. The bed beside her shifts. Lio's leaning over it, squinting, trying to read what the paper says.

"Why is this addressed to me?" Ayne bellows—rage clawing across her face. "And there's another too." She moves aside the next piece of paper to reveal the second letter from Talin. "All along, you've been reading and keeping *my* letters?" She slaps the stack of paper and the quill onto the dresser, then turns and storms from the guests' quarters.

Maya groans, hurrying after her. She grabs Ayne's wrist before she can make it to the front door. "You can't go out there! They'll hurt you."

Ayne scowls, tearing her wrist from Maya's grasp. "No, they won't hurt *me*. They're after *you*, Maya. I can't believe I trusted you." She shakes her head and pivots, throwing open the door before Mason has a chance to secure a board across. Her brown eyes scan the street, where only a small portion of the crowd lingers, hands gripping fruit, vegetables, and small trinkets.

Mason sighs and drops the board and nail he's holding—now unable to board the door shut since Ayne just left.

"Where are you going to go?" Maya demands, crossing her arms.

Ayne tilts her head high and scoffs. "Somewhere away from you." Then she disappears into the small crowd.

Maya doesn't move to watch her go. She doesn't move at all until Mason wraps his arms around her. She doesn't realize she's shaking, that tears are dripping down her face until he wipes them away. An orchestra of *thud, thud, thud* envelopes them as the crowd outside pelts her house.

"What's the matter, Maya?" he whispers, delicately, like the slightest sound will break her.

Maya sniffles, her vision is blurry and her throat is tight. "Ayne left..." She already knows that he's aware of that, but she can't find enough courage to say anything else.

She can't see his face—she doesn't want to see his face. Would he blame her for driving Ayne away? For putting Ayne in danger?

"Oh," he mutters, smoothing back her hair. "I'll go find her." He kisses the top of her head and gently leads her to the couch. "I'll be back soon, okay?"

Maya stares numbly at the unlit fireplace. She nods. As soon as he leaves, she collapses.

She knows it was wrong, but she had to keep her word to King Ren. If Ayne saw those letters before the trade routes closed, then she'd insist on going home. And then, she wasn't half as good of a witch as she is now.

Bao scurries across the floor and hops up on the couch. He sits beside Maya, nuzzling his face into the crook of her neck.

"I love you too," Maya mumbles, wringing her hands.

And then a loud *boom* shakes her house and the sound of the crowd outside fades away.

She spins around, staring out her window as a black plume of smoke descends over her street. The food market across from her house is engulfed in flames. The thick smoke crawls underneath her door. She watches it creep across the floor, closer and closer...

She shouts, "Lio! Leave the house, it isn't safe anymore!" Each word is laced with urgency, but that's all she can manage to get out before the smoke reaches her. It wraps around her throat, envelops her body—she chokes. She doubles over, coughing.

Bao falls to the floor next to her.

Maya can hear the sound of footsteps running through the house. She reaches over and caresses Bao's tiny face before her world turns black.

CHAPTER TWENTY-THREE

The Courtier

Maya's eyes snap open and she bolts upright. She instantly reaches for Bao, not even looking to see who woke her up. Bao coughs, but crawls into her arms, allowing her to cradle him.

Then she looks over her shoulder. Mason's staring straight at her. His eyes are puffy red and his cheeks are streaked with black ash that clung to his sweat.

He extends a hand toward her, sweeping a lock of hair away from her face and pushing it behind her ear. "Maya, are you okay?"

His words are soft—sweet and unsure.

She offers him a small smile. "Yes," she croaks, "I think I'll be fine."

He helps her up, wrapping an arm around her waist. "We need to get out of here," he says, even though the thick smoke is trying to choke him too.

He finds the door in the darkness and begins to fumble around for the knob. He locates it, and throws the door open, exposing them to the chaos outside.

Maya takes a raggedy breath in. The fresh air feels like it's scorching her lungs.

The entire street in front of her is on fire. A sound close to rampaging animals draws her attention up the street.

A large swath of people with torches, spears, and bows, are gathered. They're storming through the town, their voices are loud and clear, even above all the commotion.

"Give us Maya Lee!" they shout, lifting their weapons high. "Anyone who dares side with the emperor must be brought to justice! We cannot let him gain an even bigger advantage on us! We will not stand by and let him destroy our country!"

Mason turns back to Maya, his face is grave. "They don't know where you live..." he says, raising his eyebrows. "Which means we need to go *now* before they find out." He looks back inside the house. "Where's Lio?"

Maya coughs, waving the lingering smoke away from her face. It's getting even darker, thicker, as the rebels light even more things on fire. "I told her to go. I heard her go."

"We need to find her," he says, directing her to a path alongside her house.

"Did you find Ayne?"

Mason shakes his head, then realizing that she can hardly see—says, "No. I heard the explosion and saw the fire. It was too close to you, I couldn't let you get hurt."

Maya frowns, resting her hand on his that's around her waist. She stifles back another cough. "But Ayne could be in danger..."

"Ayne can defend herself..." His words are rough and scratchy. The fire is getting to him too. "But we should find her soon. With all this smoke, and all those people, she won't be able to defend herself for long."

"Where are we going?" Maya asks, trying to decipher the darkness.

"To the ports. We need to go back to Gaia."

Maya stops in her tracks, forcing him to stop as well. "We'll never be able to get a ride—and besides, I can't just leave my home." Her hand searches for Bao's, seeking the comfort of her companion's grip. She doesn't find it. Her words come out blurred together, desperate, terrified, "He's not here. Bao! Bao!" Maya runs back the way she came, slipping from Mason's arms. She stumbles, scraping her knees against the gravel, tearing her dress. She doesn't care. Not when the thing she cares the most about is lost. "Bao!"

She extends her hands in both directions, feeling her way back home. Something warm and soft grazes her cheek—a slight plume of warm air against her palm. Her eyes widen and she spins in that direction. She finds him slumped against her house, eyes closed, and breathing weakly.

She cradles Bao, pressing his face against her chest, trying to protect him from the annihilating smoke. A hand finds her. Warm, protective; it tugs on her arm, pulling her forward. Her feet slip on the gravel road; Mason pulls her back up. They keep going. She falls again, slamming into the ground, rolling to protect Bao. Her throat closes, hot tears stream down her cheeks, one petrifying thought echoes through her mind: *what if this is it? What if this is how I die?*

Mason wraps an arm around her shoulders, another around her legs. He heaves her up and continues through the smoke. Bao rests curled in her arms.

Gray penetrates the seemingly endless black—the gray of a smoggy sky.

The sound of waves, shouts, and bird calls, grows increasingly louder with each step he takes. They burst through the cloud of smoke and stumble onto the dock.

A line of ships bounces on the current. He runs, calling for a captain. No one replies.

Maya looks up, her eyelids feel heavy, everything feels heavy. She can hear Mason's frantic shouts and the deafening quiet that comes after. She can hear her hope start to fade.

"Yeah?" a man says. His voice is gravelly and deep. He has an immaculately trimmed beard, short yet full. He's tall. Taller than both of them. And he's standing on the deck of a large ship that's definitely Zhongguo made. Navy-colored boards with white details. In elegant cursive across the side of the ship in the Common language is the ship's name: *Last Hope*.

CHAPTER TWENTY-FOUR

The Captain

Maya wraps her hands around the warm mug offered to her by the captain. She's sitting inside his cabin at the very back of the ship, waiting for Mason to get back with the two girls.

His room, much like everything else, is navy and white. A barnacle-clad anchor hangs on the wall above his bed, a torch sconce on both sides.

The captain sits down on the stool next to her, a small round table separates them. He sets his mug down; the scent of mint is strong and makes her stomach growl.

She takes a sip—the warmth soothes her coarse throat. She hadn't realized it before—but her hands are shaking. The tea ripples against the mug. She sets it down.

The captain looks at her—a look she can't decipher. "Are you the one they are searching for?" His Zhongguonese accent is heavy, making the Common language melodic.

He doesn't seem particularly hostile. He did take her in after all. She bites her lip. Her eyes flit around, trying to find something to focus on that's not him. She lands on the anchor, tracing the unique edges as she forms her next words. "And if I am?"

He nods slowly, taking a drink of his tea. "If you are, then it is not safe for you here. The rebels will not stop. They will destroy anyone who sides with the emperor."

She shrinks at the thought. Her homeland isn't safe? She imagines her house igniting, the walls she is so accustomed to...crumbling. Nikolai's home. His painting...

A lone tear rolls over her cheek, paving a way through the grime.

The captain tilts his head, studying her with narrowed eyes. "I will take you away from here."

She's too numb to be surprised. "I don't want to go. This is my home." She looks up at him, trying in vain to understand him. "Would you leave your homeland?"

He shrugs. "I would leave if I knew it wasn't safe." He waves a hand toward the doorway where the world outside is burning.

She goes back to studying the anchor, finding comfort in how it's so easy to understand. It was once used. Now it's not.

The captain she can't understand. He's willing to disobey direct orders from the emperor, for *her?* A witch. A woman wanted by a band of rebels for nothing more than saving her friend, and herself, from the emperor. He doesn't even know her. Why is he so willing to help? What is he getting out of it? Maya's thoughts are loud in her mind, demanding answers.

He leans over the table. His voice is quiet. "I'll take you wherever you want…for a price. You can pay me when we get there."

She sighs, relief flooding through her veins. So that's what he wants—that's why he's doing this—

money.

He raises an eyebrow. "We'll have to leave soon. All this attention has probably drawn the eye of the emperor. I refuse to be caught up with all this, especially with you, so we better hurry."

Maya nods, drinking her remaining tea. Her hand has stilled. An option, an option she's never been granted before: to create a new life for herself. A new identity, perhaps. Where she isn't known as the witch. Where she's known as what she wants to be, not what she was born as.

An option has never enticed her so much before.

Yet, she can feel the dread—the dread change usually brings. It's a strange feeling swirling inside her chest; hope for a new life and sorrow for the one she's leaving behind.

There are shouts on the dock. Hooves beat sadistically. People scream. Fire crackles.

The captain opens the door, watching the scene outside unfold. He mutters a Zhongguonese curse word under his breath and slams the door closed. When he turns to her, his eyes are quick and panicked.

"What is it?" Maya demands, standing from the table. She narrows her eyes at the captain. "Tell me."

"They're here," he states, scowling.

"Mason? Does he have the two girls?"

He nods. "Yes, but *they're* here as well."

Maya slams a flat palm onto the table. "Now is not the time for guessing games. Elaborate."

He huffs. "The emperor's calvary. They're here."

CHAPTER TWENTY-FIVE

The Sacrifice

Maya turns to Bao, gesturing to the bed. "You need to stay here, Bao. Hide." He reaches for her hand, his large black eyes begging her to stay. She shakes her head. Tears prick behind her eyes, threatening to emerge. She frowns, kissing the top of his head. "It's hard for me to leave you too, Bao. But I'll be back. Just hide…in case…"

He hugs her. A hug telling her everything he wants her to know: *I love you. Please come back.*

Maya doesn't let go of his hand as he clambers to the bed, tucking himself underneath it, not until his hand slips from hers.

"Be safe, my son," she whispers. With one last look at Bao, at his small face peeking out from the shadows, she turns to the door and to the emperor's fleet: gold and crimson-clad horses. Warriors with recurve bows drawn, metal arrowheads glinting in the few rays of the sun. Their hooves thundering against the ground. Mason, Lio, and Ayne's arms swing ferociously as they run.

Determination marking them all.

Ayne's first to make it to the dock. Her feet hit the wood boards. She slips, falls, and picks herself up again. She slams across the dock, eyes searching for pale skin, short black hair, and a crimson dress.

Maya steps off the ship. Ayne skids to a stop in front of her. She's panting. Ash is thick on her face. "Go," Maya demands, pushing Ayne onto the ship. "Go to the room. Back there!" She points and Ayne charges onward. She doesn't look back.

The warriors are gaining on them. Horses are always faster than people.

An arrow slices through the air, sticking with a thud in the dock boards beside Lio's feet. She screams, dodges it, and presses on.

Another arrow. Another miss.

Mason tears across the dock, gliding effortlessly past Lio. He stops, draws back, wraps a hand around her waist, and surges onward. He's slower now.

The horses grow closer. Another arrow loosens. It hits its target.

Mason slams into the dock, the shaft of a gold arrow protrudes from his back. A scream rips through the air. Maya doesn't realize it came from her until she's running forward, ignoring her cascading tears, only stopping when she reaches him. Lio hesitates, eyes wide, fright dancing across her face, but she charges toward the ship where Ayne is at. Maya embraces Mason, sweeping his sweaty hair off his forehead. The horses close in around them. The warriors look down, grim satisfaction mirrored on all their faces.

Maya doesn't stop herself. Her magic, pink and fiery, rages around them. She boils water from the Cari and sends it splashing against the warriors.

Some fall, twitching with agony as the water burns their flesh. Others poise their gleaming golden helmets to protect themselves, receiving only a few drops.

Another stampede of hooves echoes from the

burning city. The emperor parts through the surrounding warriors, atop a beautiful black Gypsy horse. Red and gold tassels dangle from the saddle. He glares down at her, yet a smile still plays on his face. "Maya Lee. You know this is all because of you, yes? You should've used that power of yours to stop them before they burned my city to the ground. In the act of not-acting, you allowed this to happen." He shakes his head, chuckling menacingly. "Take her to my dungeon. Take him too."

"And what about the others?" a warrior asks, turning to face the emperor.

The emperor glares down at Maya as he says, "We've got what we need right here. Let them go."

Maya makes only one wish as she stares at the emperor: that the captain makes good on his word, and whisks Ayne, Lio, Bao, Caz, and the little brown gerbil away, taking them somewhere safe.

CHAPTER TWENTY-SIX

The Guard

Maya sits in the middle of her cell, glaring at the guard that's keeping watch. He doesn't seem to care, which infuriates her.

"Is he okay?" she asks, for the millionth time since they locked her up—taking Mason somewhere else in the palace. Her only hope is that they took him to the infirmary. That they're going to help him. That he'll be okay.

The guard doesn't move. Doesn't say anything.

She groans and claws her fingers through her hair.

She needs answers.

She only looks up when another guard walks by her cell, stopping to talk to the current one.

He nods in her direction. "Is she okay? Mentally, I mean."

They laugh, making a slightly feral growl rip from Maya's throat.

"I have news from the emperor," the new guard says, more quietly, leaning closer to his comrade.

She draws from the shadows encasing her, remembering a simple hearing spell—one that she's only used once. She crosses her fingers, hoping it'll work. Her mind feels fuzzy. Her ears pop. Then she can hear *everything*: a cricket chirping in the palace gardens. The soft prayers of the prisoner beside her. The guard's words.

"Emperor Neo has pulled out of the war with Gaia. Word is, he's now joining forces."

"Really? Why would he do that?"

"I don't know. There's supposedly a huge threat against Zhongguo, and Klymora and Gaia offered to assist him if he disbanded his plan."

"And he did?"

"Yeah." The guard shrugs. "Guess it's really big.

Emperor Neo always gets what he wants... I'm kind of scared to find out what the huge threat is. There are rumors of Rutheria looking for some kind of flower that can heal anything. Allegedly that flower is here."

She presses her mouth shut. She can't say anything—even though there's so much to say. A threat made by Rutheria, a country that's avoided waging wars throughout the centuries?

Another guard joins them. He has excellent posture. A rigid chin. Thick, tousled hair poking out from underneath a helmet. He says something to them...something she strangely can't hear, which should be impossible since she's using magic. The two guards shrug and leave, continuing their conversation in hushed tones.

The new guard takes up their former position. He keeps his eyes lowered to the ground, hiding his face from her view.

Even more irritating than the first guard, at least he looked at her.

"Do you know if he's okay? The man with the arrow—the one brought in with me," she tries, refusing to acknowledge that answers probably wouldn't be given.

The guard looks up at her. The only thing she can see underneath the brim of his helmet are two piercing, magnificent eyes…

Two blue eyes. The same blue eyes she stared at every day when she went to sleep, and every day when she woke up.

"Nikolai?" she mutters…his name sounds foreign on her lips, like it's knocking the dust of his absence away.

"I'm back, my love," he whispers, giving her a small smile that barrels straight into her heart.

END of BOOK 2

Acknowledgments

If you're reading this, I assume you've read the first book in the series as well...and therefore you've earned my immense gratitude. If you enjoyed *The Empire's Witch*, I'd love it if you left a review on any platform of your choosing—reviews are the best way to help an author.

Now, for the acknowledgments...

Jacob, this literally wouldn't be done without you. Thank you for being my efficient and brilliant editor—and for putting up with my endless questions.

Nonni, thank you for reading everything I've written—and for treasuring my very first manuscript...even though it's chock-full of plot holes and spelling errors. And, thank you for all the time and energy you dedicated to *The Heiress of Gaia*. I'm not sure my appreciation comes off in person—but I am immensely grateful. I seriously wouldn't be a published author if it wasn't for you.

Mom... I'm not sure there are the right words to describe what you are to me. But I'll try; you're a true, honest friend. A confidant. One of the funniest people I know. You're talented and hard-working, and you inspire me every day. I know all your stories are going to be bestsellers. (Let's just say Smeagle is clairvoyant and he tells me things.)

Sydney… There are many things I could say about you, and I won't lie and say they're all good, but you're so incredibly creative and talented, and even though you only get spurts of energy to work on projects and you don't always finish them—what you do get done is always astounding. Keep being you (maybe a less annoying version of yourself, if I'm being honest, but you nonetheless.) (P.s. She's my sister so I'm allowed to tease her.)

And Papa, thanks so much for all you do. Most, however, aren't related to my writing, though you're very supportive in that department as well. But thanks for all the little things. The random memes throughout the day, the spine-breaking hugs, and the countless inside jokes. There's nobody like you, that's for sure.

About the Author

Daphne Paige has always loved writing; watching and learning from her mother, who's also a writer. With the majority of her time spent writing, the breaks between stories makes her remember she has an actual life away from her characters.
During those breaks, she loves to play video games, hangout with her various pets, and watch classic black and white films with her family.
Daphne lives in Oregon helping her family with their popcorn business.

Photo credit: Sydney Marie
@sydneymariewatercolor on Instagram

More By the Author

The Heiress of Gaia (January 2022)
The Empire's Witch (December 2022)
Jess (April 2023)

Made in the USA
Middletown, DE
03 January 2023